MW01063806

DETOUR

Cover design by: Hang Le
www.byhangle.com/

Photographed by and copyright owned by: Regina Wamba
www.reginawamba.com

Editing and formatting by: Elaine York,
Allusion Graphics, LLC/Publishing & Book Formatting
www.allusiongraphics.com

Ebook interior images by Christine Borgford

Proofreading & copyediting by: Bethany Salminen
www.bethanyedits.net

THE
GETAWAY
SERIES

DETOUR

NEW YORK TIMES BESTSELLING AUTHOR
JAY CROWNOVER

Dedicated to love.
However that looks. In all its different forms.
Everyone should be so lucky to find the kind of love that is powerful
enough to both hurt and heal.

Foreword:

I didn't know I was going to get this far in the *Getaway* series!

I wrote *Retreat* on a whim to stretch my writerly wings. I didn't plan on folks taking to the Warners the way they did, and I didn't know that I was going to become low-key obsessed with writing about Rodie and Wyatt.

This is my disclaimer to folks who might actually live and love near Sheridan, Wyoming. Since the town was just the backdrop in the other novels, I didn't think I needed to make it a fictional place. I used a real town on the map, which I normally only do if I am *very* familiar with the place and people I'm writing about. Since Sheridan played a tiny part in the previous novels, I kept the Warner Ranch near a real place on the Wyoming/Montana border. *However*, I didn't realize what a big part the city and residents of my fictional version of Sheridan were going to play in the story when I got to Rodie and Wyatt's book.

I'm sure the good folks of Sheridan are lovely, open-minded, incredibly empathetic and understanding people in real life. In my fictional Sheridan, that isn't the case. So, I feel like I need to clarify: the locals and the situations that arise in the *Getaway* series are entirely fictional. The town is also considerably bigger than I make it seem in this series. I tweaked the perception to fit my previous narrative.

So, I apologize for taking liberties with Sheridan and the folks who call it home. There was just no way to adjust the location this far into the series. (The previous two books in the series take place on the road, so I had to bring everyone home in this book!) Just know, any inaccuracies or generalizations relating to this very real place are my own and in no way reflect the reality of what I'm positive is a lovely town in cowboy country.

I feel like I owe the real Sheridan a visit after this series is all wrapped up!

XOXO
Love & Ink,
Jay

PROLOGUE

WYATT

I SAW HIM AS SOON as I stepped off the plane in Billings, Montana. The airport wasn't huge, but I would've spotted him in a crowd if it was. It annoyed me to no end that I couldn't miss Rodie Collins. The sheriff of the small Wyoming town where my younger brother had settled down had been irritatingly unforgettable since the moment we met well over a year ago. It got under my skin and made my back teeth grind furiously when I realized that others weren't immune to the intimidating man's larger-than-life presence. The young mother in front of me, who had been frazzled and loud the entire flight, missed a step and nearly sent her toddler flying when she caught sight of the tall, auburn-haired man. He pushed off the wall where he was leaning so he could make his way toward our gate. I heard her inhale a sharp breath, and I couldn't contain an eye roll. Sure, there was no getting around the fact that Rodie Collins was one hell of a good-looking man, but there was something hard and unforgiving in his green gaze that warned everyone to keep a safe distance. If the coldness in his eyes weren't enough to make anyone with a functioning brain leery, the badge and gun on his belt would be.

For most of my adult life, I'd had a badge and gun of my own. I shouldn't be impressed by Rodie's, but I was. Righteousness and authority looked good on the man, and even though I'd die before admitting it out loud, I was jealous. The only way I'd get my badge back was if I agreed to a desk job for the remainder of my career. And no one could give me an honest answer as to whether or not I'd ever be able to fire a gun properly again. My shoulder had been blown into too many pieces to count on my last undercover assignment, rendering me virtually useless in the eyes of the law. I'd barely gotten feeling back in the injured limb, let alone full mobility. I was never exactly thrilled to see the stoic sheriff, but encountering him when I was beaten down and as close to giving up on everything in my life as I'd ever been, well, this was pretty much my own private version of Hell on Earth. And the very handsome devil was now staring in my direction.

As the young mother continued to gawk at the tall man in the black cowboy hat and tan uniform, I narrowed my eyes and leaned heavily on the cane in my hand. My shoulder hadn't been the only part of my body that was nearly destroyed in the ambush down by the border. In fact, it was nearly a miracle I was still walking, talking, and breathing. None of the doctors who'd fought to keep me alive after I was airlifted to a hospital in San Antonio could promise that I'd ever be able to function like I used to again. None of them knew how stubborn and determined I could be. However, Rodie didn't seem to be shocked at all that I was making my way on my own two unsteady feet.

"Where's Webb?" My younger brother had been harassing me for months to come stay with him in Wyoming at the sprawling ranch where he worked. He insisted the fresh air would do me good, and the wide-open space would be the perfect place to figure out my next step in life. I'd scared him big time when this last assignment went so bad, and he wasn't about to let me forget it. He also wasn't going to let me forget that I'd gone from being a highly decorated soldier to being a highly decorated DEA agent. I'd always lived a life with no ties and no guarantees, and now I was at a total loss as to what to do with myself. Honestly, I was confused as to who I was supposed to be without my badge and a dangerous mission to complete. "He was supposed to come pick me up."

Webb had to know that the last person I wanted to make the two-hour drive out to the ranch with was the man currently standing in front of me. I'd mentioned to both Webb and his pretty girlfriend that something about the sheriff of Sheridan rubbed me the wrong way.

"He said he was caught up with one of the tours on the ranch, and Ten is out tracking a missing hiker." One broad shoulder lifted and fell totally unbothered. "Ten radioed in and asked me to come pick you up. Gotta keep up with the 'serve' part of 'protect and serve.'" One corner of his mouth lifted and I narrowed my eyes to hide the fact that his lopsided grin made my heart thud heavily in my bruised and healing chest.

"None of the brothers could come and get me?"

The ranch my brother called home was owned and operated by the Warner family. The brothers were lifelong Wyoming residents and true-blue cowboys. The family was great. I was endlessly appreciative of how they'd all taken Webb in and made him part of the family. Especially since our childhood had been garbage and traumatic as hell for both of us. No one deserved a sense of security and a place to belong more than Webb. His girlfriend, Tennyson McKenna, was also from the area around Sheridan and she seemed just as tough as the terrain. She was my brother's perfect match and the only person I trusted to love him the way he deserved. She wasn't going anywhere, no matter how the world tried to challenge them, and that was what my brother needed more than anything.

"What can I say? Everyone was busy, so you're stuck with me." The grin on Rodie's ruggedly handsome face widened, and something sparked in his emerald gaze. My instincts were honed to a fine edge from years of working undercover in some of the most dangerous places in the world, and the hair on the back of my neck lifted as something about Rodie's easy willingness to play chauffeur didn't sit quite right. Every alarm bell I possessed was ringing loud enough to drown out the rest of the sounds around us.

"I could've arranged for a car service. I'm sure you're busy keeping the people of Sheridan safe." I couldn't keep the bite of sarcasm out of my tone. Sheridan was a small town in middle-of-nowhere Wyoming. I knew that Rodie had been a Recon Marine in his former life. But I didn't know how he ended up keeping the peace in a place you had to look pretty hard to find. The big man had clearly taken a step down from what he was capable of. It should be common knowledge that he was way overqualified for his current position considering his training.

I grimaced in pain. I could stand on my own, but not for extended periods of time. Our standoff was zapping the last of my energy, and my shoulder was starting to scream at me. I needed a painkiller and a nap. I didn't need a silent face-off against a man I was going to lose to anyway. Rodie was bigger than I was, and taller. He was a few years older than me, but he looked like he was ten years younger. There wasn't a single stray strand of silver or white in his thick auburn hair, and his body looked like he could play for the nearest professional sports team. Before my last mission went bad, I'd like to think I kept myself in pretty good shape and could hold my own in the looks department. Rodie didn't hold his own; he dominated the department and made me feel even worse. I knew I looked as rough as I felt. It was just one more reason I didn't want to be stuck in a car with him for two hours. I already had a complex about this guy; I didn't need to add another one.

Rodie's mahogany eyebrows lifted and I swore he was fighting back a full smile. "Come on. You clearly need to get off your feet. You look like you're ready to pass out. You can continue being disgruntled that I'm your ride once we get in the car. How many bags do we have to grab from baggage claim?" I should've known he wasn't going to respond to my comment about the car service. It was stupid and made me sound ungrateful and petty. It would cost a fortune to get me to the ranch, so I should just shut it and be happy I didn't have to hitchhike.

I rubbed my free fingers across my forehead and tried to will away the rising headache. "A couple." All my earthly belongings fit in both, which was sad and spoke more about my own personal state than anything. It was another reason Webb demanded I come recuperate in Wyoming. My brother was worried I'd completely lost myself in my job, and he very well may have been right. It shouldn't have taken me less than an hour to leave my entire life behind, yet it did.

The burgeoning smile quickly died and the brightness in those jade eyes hardened. I felt a chill shoot up my spine as Rodie's perceptive gaze dragged up and down the entire length of my battered body.

"Who helped you get to the airport in DC? There's no way you managed to wrangle a couple of bags in your condition." Those dark eyebrows furrowed and his head tilted down, the brim of his cowboy hat casting his face in a slight shadow. Something was obviously bothering him. "Are you leaving someone special behind? Is that why you kept telling Webb and Ten no when they asked you to come to Wyoming?"

The questions didn't feel like a friendly inquiry. There was something darker, more demanding underneath them. If I weren't worried about falling on my ass, I would've tried to take a step back. Suddenly, I felt like Rodie was doing his best to crowd me, to take up all the space and air around me. Or maybe I was just so hyper-aware of him I simply couldn't see or feel anything beyond him.

I held up my hand on my good side and cleared my throat, trying for some semblance of control in the situation. "There is no one special. I'm not leaving anyone behind. Grady came down from New York to help me get everything together and take me to the airport." My former partner in the DEA was the one who got my DC condo ready to sell as well. He was also the one who walked me through Dulles, holding tight to my arm, like I was some kind of invalid. Grady was the only person I trusted, aside from Wyatt. The only person besides my brother I could abide seeing how truly weak and damaged I was.

Almost instantly, the brewing agitation in Rodie's gaze cleared, and the chill that had slipped over my skin lifted. The man across from me was powerful without even trying, and I hated that I reacted to his mere expressions so quickly. I tried to keep myself composed, but something about the small-town sheriff got under my skin and stayed there.

Without another word, Rodie turned on the heel of his boot and led the way toward the tiny baggage claim. He obviously slowed his typically distance-eating stride in consideration of my much slower and unsteady gait. I was glad the airport was small. By the time we got to baggage claim, I was exhausted and twice as shaky on my feet.

The strain of the walk must've shown on my face, because as soon as we came across a bench, Rodie pointed to an empty seat and ordered, "Sit."

I scowled at him, my hand tightening defensively around the handle of my cane. "Am I a dog?" Taking orders had never been my strong suit, and everything inside me balked at how badly I wanted to simply listen to him.

Rodie heaved a sigh and rolled his eyes. Pushing the brim of his hat back with a single finger, he leaned down slightly so we were eye-to-eye. I felt my breath catch and my heart start to pound. It was a lot to have all that intensity focused directly on me. It wasn't good for my peace of mind to be this close to someone I was undeniably attracted to, but knew without a doubt *could never* and *would never* return those feelings. I'd stopped having one-sided crushes on cute, straight boys when I was a teenager. It'd only taken getting my heart crushed once to learn that lesson.

"Sit your ass down, Special Agent Bryant, or I will put you on that bench and make sure you don't get up." I felt my jaw drop at the quiet demand. Stunned and speechless, I practically collapsed into the seat as I continued to stare up at the sheriff. I slowly turned cherry red from embarrassment or because I was turned on, I wasn't sure which. Rodie grinned down at me and flashed a wink that brought an unchecked growl from my throat. "Good boy. Now tell me what your bags look like so I can grab them for you."

Feeling disoriented and numb, I just blinked up at the other man, forcing him to repeat his question several times. Rodie got frustrated at my lack of response and reached out a hand to grab my chin. He forced my head back, making me meet his unwavering gaze. "Come on, pretty boy. Tell me what I'm looking for so I can get you out of here and into a nice, soft bed. If you faint on me and I have to throw you over my shoulder to get you out to the car, I'm going to kick your ass."

Holy hell. The combination of his touch and the visuals that assaulted my senses was breathtaking. I apparently took too long to answer because he grunted, reminding me he was awaiting my response.

"Oh, uh, look for two matching gray Samsonite bags." I gave my head a shake and narrowed my eyes up at him. "Don't make fun of me when I can't fight back."

I watched Rodie's eyes widen as he straightened, his hold on my chin tightening. "Make fun of you? What in the hell are you talking about?" His deep voice changed to an angry rumble.

I swatted at the hand holding my face, trying to get him to back off. "Pretty boy. I may have been at one point, but we both know that's no longer the case. I'm well aware I look like someone who survived being tossed in a wood chipper."

He made a sound deep and low in his broad chest and took a step closer to me. I could feel the tension vibrating off his big body, and I shifted anxiously on the uncomfortable bench.

A shocked gasp escaped my lips when the pad of Rodie's thumb suddenly slid across the curve of my bottom lip. I literally stopped breathing at his touch. The warmth of his hand disappeared a second later as he finally fell back a step and put some space between us.

"You're alive, Special Agent. That's a beautiful thing, no matter who's looking at it. And you..." He shook his head slightly and turned when the conveyor belt with the luggage started moving. "Pretty sure it'll take more than a couple of bullet holes and a cane to make you anything other than pretty."

He didn't have to push through the crowd to get to the front of the group. They automatically parted for him. I was left staring at his wide back, the muscles there stretching his ugly uniform to its limits. I shook my head and lifted a shaking hand to touch my lips.

I had no idea what game Rodie was playing with me, but I didn't like it. He already had my insides tied in knots whenever I was around him. But this was something else entirely. My insides were bursting into flames, and he was stoking the fire. I never kept my sexuality a secret, but it wasn't something I advertised or openly discussed with anyone who wasn't in my inner circle. There were a lot of interesting things about me; who I slept with didn't even top the list most days.

When she was alive, my mother had hated me and the fact I was gay. She went out of her way to make sure I knew how disappointed and disgusted she was in me. The military was also less than open-minded, no matter how much progress had been made in recent years. The DEA was another organization that had some pretty tricky social standards to navigate when it came to being open and upfront about an agent's private life. My entire life, I'd kept quiet unless asked directly, which was a policy that had always worked well for me. However, Rodie definitely knew that I was gay. He'd overheard a conversation I'd had with a confused and miserable teenager not too long ago. He was a lost and alone young man one of the Warner brothers brought home who needed a sympathetic ear. The poor kid really thought being gay was the end of the road for him, and that it was the reason his short life had been so tragic. He honestly thought that he had no job prospects or options other than selling his body on the streets.

I'd promised him that being gay didn't mean a damn thing in the long run if you were qualified and worked hard. I told him to stop defining himself by his sexuality and to start defining himself as the kind, caring young man he was. I didn't realize Rodie was lurking around the corner for the duration of the conversation. I expected some kind of judgment from the aggressively masculine sheriff. He reminded me so much of the guys I used to serve with back in the day. None of them had been known for their tolerance and understanding. Rodie already thought that those of us from the city had no place in his western oasis. But, to my surprise, he never said a word; he simply asked the teenager to let him know if he had any problems and promised that he wouldn't tolerate bullying or discrimination in Sheridan, regardless of the situation.

So, Rodie had to know when he touched me the way he did, I'd read into it.

Sulking and quickly succumbing to the pain flowing through every limb and nerve, I spaced out and slumped down on the bench. It had been a long ass day and my mind and body were shutting down. That had to be why I was freaking out over this situation. It had to be.

I had no idea how much time passed, but it felt like only seconds later when a wide hand slapped down on my shoulder and roughly shook me awake. My eyes snapped open and I was face-to-face with Rodie. He looked concerned and slightly pissed off.

"Exactly how badly are you hurt, Wyatt? Do we need to take you to the ER before hitting the road?" His eyes roved over me, and I could see worry stamped clearly on his face.

I flicked his hand away, and slowly, painstakingly, climbed to my feet. "I'm fine. Or I will be. I'm going to take a painkiller and sleep once we get to the car. You don't need to worry about me, Sheriff."

Rodie manhandled my two suitcases as I followed him toward the airport exit. I was lost in thought, struggling to stay upright, when I thought I heard him mutter, "But I do, Special Agent."

I convinced myself I was just overly tired and in too much pain to be thinking clearly. I needed my medication and some sleep. There was no way this bossy, grumpy, straitlaced cowboy was wasting a single second thinking about me in any kind of personal way.

I refused to let myself fall for such an unrealistic fantasy.

CHAPTER 1

RODIE

STUPID, STUBBORN MAN.

No one, and I mean *no one*, got under my skin and riled me up like Wyatt Bryant.

He refused to use the cane—that he'd been clutching like a lifeline when he got off the plane—in front of his younger brother. He was stubborn, and his pride was going to land him on his ass at Webb's feet before the day was over. I watched him nearly fall over twice when he shook me off, and I could hear the way his breathing went ragged when he tried to manhandle his suitcases out of my service vehicle. He was too proud to ask for help, and too hard-headed to give in when assistance was forced on him. He wasn't behaving like someone who'd nearly died on the operating table a couple of months ago. He was acting like someone who had yet to accept their new limitations and refused to settle into their new normal.

When we first met, I hated everything about his suave, slick, metropolitan demeanor. I could tell he thought my position as sheriff in my small town was beneath him. He flashed that federal badge of his in my face every single time our paths crossed, and as a result, we butted heads and exchanged sharp words on a fairly regular basis. I always called him 'city boy,' more to remind myself there was an unbridgeable gap that existed between the two of us than to annoy him, but his prickly reaction to the nickname was always fun to watch. Only today, I hadn't wanted to poke and prod at the man when he was so obviously still on the mend, both mentally and physically. Instead, I had the nearly overwhelming urge to take care of him, to coddle him and shelter him from all the really nasty shit guys in our line of work had to go through regularly. Being a law enforcement officer was no joke, and it really sucked when you were cast out, after years of service and sacrifice, just because your body gave out on you. It wasn't fair, and it was easy to see the heartbreak and betrayal Wyatt was still processing. There were multiple levels of pain radiating out of the man's periwinkle eyes.

So, when I accidentally let it slip how pretty I thought he was, I decided to own it. I knew he wouldn't believe the words anyway, and he would just write them off as another annoying nickname. Wyatt tended to focus on how much we didn't have in common and blatantly ignore the things we did. Since the former DEA agent was determined to turn a blind eye to the obvious attraction I had toward him, I had no other choice but to make my intentions clear to his younger brother. Webb and Wyatt were close. I knew anything I said to one was going to get back to the other. Once I'd dropped a veritable bomb at Webb's feet by telling him, in no uncertain terms, that I wanted to help Wyatt loosen some of that rigid control he held onto so tightly, I knew the message was bound to make it to him sooner or later.

I left Webb, who was looking slightly alarmed at my interest in his brother, feeling undeniably pleased with myself. Satisfied Wyatt was in good hands, I radioed my station to let them know I was on the way back into town. The Warner's ranch was located well outside of Sheridan, as were most of the sprawling properties that had been in the local families for generations. It wasn't a quick trip to get anywhere in the area, but luckily Sheridan was a pretty quiet town, and my staff was self-sufficient when I had other obligations. We rarely had the kind of major crime that required the sheriff to be hands-on. It was mostly stupid petty crime and public disturbances at the height of tourist season.

When I first came back to Wyoming after the service, I didn't have any plans to stay.

In fact, I'd been in a situation very similar to Wyatt's. I thought I was going to be a career soldier; I was planning to serve my country until I was too old or killed in action. I was devoted, good at my job, and didn't have any family or significant other waiting for me back home. Only, no one told me that I needed a backup plan in case I was only *nearly* killed in action but somehow managed to pull through. Near death, bitter and angry at the world, I didn't have much choice but to take a former commanding officer up on his offer to go back to Sheridan and recuperate. I never planned on returning to my small hometown, but here I was.

Sheridan hadn't been easy on my mother when she showed up as a pregnant teenager. My father was nonexistent, and my mother's aunt and uncle took her in and begrudgingly raised both of us. They were no longer around. My first commanding officer had heard me talk about my hometown enough when I was a new recruit that he became curious about the unspoiled beauty of Wyoming. I had no idea I spoke of my home with such longing after I tried so hard to leave it behind. I thought I hated the place, and all my memories of growing up were tainted and ugly. I loathed being reminded almost daily that I was nothing more than an accident and a burden. Eventually, I changed units through different promotions and deployments, and I was unaware that my first CO had retired and taken off for the wilds of Wyoming based solely on the tales I told. It wasn't until I was hurt and abandoned by the people for whom I'd nearly given my life, that I found myself back where I started.

It took almost two full years for my body to heal and for me to get my mind mostly right. In that time, I fell back in love with the wide-open spaces and wild Wyoming landscape. I was never going to be a rancher or a farmer. I was never going to work on an oil rig or be a tour guide. Luckily, by the time I was back on my feet, the local sheriff decided to retire, and my former commander encouraged me to run for his position. I had zero ties to the community, so I thought it was a long shot. Out of ideas and with no plan for my future, it was a Hail Mary that luckily paid off. With my sterling service record my former commander's endorsement, I won the election, even if it was by a very narrow margin.

It was always my main priority not to betray the trust the people of Sheridan put in me. I was an outsider, even though I grew up here, so I knew I had to work twice as hard and be extra sensitive to what the locals expected of me. That was one of the main reasons I'd yet to tell Wyatt that feeling lost after being injured on the job was only one of the things we had in common.

I was pretty sure no one in Sheridan or the surrounding area knew I was gay. I didn't talk about it. Didn't advertise it. And if I was lonely and looking for company for a couple nights, I drove to Cheyenne or even to Billings. I didn't want anyone up in my business, and I didn't want anything to rock the boat in my new life.

But, there was no getting around the fact that I was very interested in Wyatt. I was intrigued from the start and struggled to hide it. The man disappeared in the Wyoming wilderness when he went rogue on one of his assignments from the DEA. I was beyond impressed that he managed to keep himself alive in the harsh terrain, and that he somehow managed to evade an entire cartel network for weeks with no backup. He brought down the entire syndicate with the help of his brother, his former partner, and the Warner brothers, all while acting like it was just another day on the job. It was rare to encounter someone so dedicated to justice at any cost and so cool in any situation.

Not long after the incident in the mountains, both Webb and Wyatt had to face the sudden appearance of a long-lost brother neither knew about. Webb's twin was pure evil, and he put the Bryant brothers through the wringer on multiple levels. Still, Wyatt stood by his younger brother through thick and thin, even as the truth of their terrible childhood and horrible upbringing threatened to tear them apart. The guy was a rock, reliable and unwavering. I found his loyalty and determination to be there for those he loved incredibly endearing and attractive.

I liked his polished look. Pretty boys weren't typically my thing, but Wyatt looked like a slightly damaged Disney prince with his golden hair, tinted with just a hint of silver in the thick strands. His eyes were the most unusual shade of bluish-purple, like the wildflowers that grew in the fields surrounding the town. He looked every inch the special agent, and all I wanted to do was ruffle his perfectly styled hair and make his one-of-a-kind eyes go hazy with lust. Wyatt Bryant had spent more time wandering in my very vivid dreams than I cared to admit.

Now that he was going to be on my turf for the foreseeable future, I was thinking maybe it was time to make those dreams a reality... as long as it was done discreetly. I wanted Wyatt, without a doubt. There was something different about him, and something different about how I felt when I was around him. Maybe it was because I was getting older. Maybe it was because I had no idea how long he was going to be in Wyoming, and I couldn't stand the thought of missing a shot with him. Something made me want to toss my regular rules out the window. But I doubted my interest in the other man would go over well with the people I was paid to protect and serve. The locals were good, hard-working people, but a solid number were far from open-minded. A gay sheriff would go over as well as rain at an outdoor wedding.

I stayed lost in thought all the way back to town, flicking a wave at whomever I passed along the way. When I got to the sheriff's station, the sun was going down and the day shift was transitioning over to the night team. I caught up on anything I missed, but it was all typical calls, nothing that was cause for concern. I gave the evening crew a short debriefing and told them I would be in my office for a few hours if anything serious popped up.

I took off my hat and tossed it on my seriously messy desk. I needed a cup of coffee and some dinner. I'd dropped everything in an embarrassingly eager manner when Ten called and asked me to get Wyatt from the airport. I was starving, but I couldn't pass up the opportunity to spend time with Wyatt one-on-one, even in his current condition. I'd take whatever I could get with that man. I was about to paw through the mess of paperwork on my desk to look for one of the few delivery menus lost in the chaos when there was a knock on my office door. It opened before I could respond to the sound, and a small, dark-haired woman immediately swept into the space.

Delaney Hall was the assistant to the mayor of Sheridan and the daughter of one of the town's wealthiest families. It wasn't uncommon for her to stop by during business hours, even during non-business hours. She and her husband had divorced recently, and it was no secret that she was looking at me to fill his place in her life and, more importantly, in her bed. I'd told her more times than I could count that I wasn't interested, but the woman was determined and not used to hearing the word 'no.'

"I've been trying to catch you all day." She flashed a smile at me. She was an attractive woman, if a little on the sharp and predatory side. I admired her ambition and her desire to help the town prosper, but we weren't friends, and I had no intention of getting close to her.

"Had some personal things to take care of. You could've just left a message and I would've called you back when I had a free minute." I dragged a hand down my face and looked at my desk. "I'm going to clean up, catch up on paperwork, grab some dinner, and head out for the night." I wasn't trying to be rude, but spending time dodging her advances was not what I considered a good time. I needed coffee and food, stat.

She made a noise and carefully used a manicured fingernail to clear one corner of my desk so she could prop her hip on its edge.

"I haven't eaten yet either. Why don't we grab something together?" The suggestion in her tone was unmistakable.

I sighed and crossed my arms over my chest. "Thanks for the offer, but I'll pass. Like I said, I still have work to do. What can I do for you this evening, Ms. Hall?"

She rolled her eyes at me and tilted her chin defiantly, something I noticed she did when I rejected her advances.

"You know the elections are coming up soon, right? The mayor wanted to make sure you know you have his endorsement, should you need it, of course." Her smile was a little too pointed for my liking. Her unspoken insinuation was pretty blatant, and I had no doubt this woman would make a terrifying enemy. It annoyed me that the mayor was riding my coattails during the elections. He hadn't done much for the town since the last elections, but he thought endorsing me would put him in a good light with the voters. He called us a team, but I could barely stand the man.

I dropped my arms and offered a careless shrug. "Last time I checked, I was running unopposed." Just like I had for the last few elections, as I'm sure she knew.

"For now. That can always change." Her dark eyebrows raised and her smile sharpened. "And you've never had to run with a body count following you before."

I grimaced and fought the urge to run a hand through my messy hair in frustration. She wasn't wrong. While Sheridan and the surrounding area tended to be peaceful, over the last year we'd had a few significant dust-ups, all of which seemed to circle around the Warner clan.

"I've always had a body count behind me." I'd been deployed to some of the most dangerous places in the world, but I couldn't escape that. "Now, only difference is that it's just a little closer to home." I sighed and moved toward the door, trying to give her the hint it was time to go. "Tell the mayor I appreciate his continued support." I couldn't honestly say it'd been a pleasure to work alongside him. He rubbed me the wrong way from the get go.

Delaney slithered from her perch and made her way over to me. She got uncomfortably close, not reading the signals that I didn't appreciate her in my personal space at all.

I flinched when she lifted a finger and pressed it against the center of my chest, her tone sounding less business and more bedroom. "What about me, Rodie? Do you appreciate my support as well? Aren't you curious just how helpful I can be?"

Biting back a growl of frustration, I reached up and caught her hand in mine. "I've told you, I don't mix work and play. I keep my professional and personal life very separate. I'm flattered that you're interested in me, but like I've said on more than one occasion, I have no inclination to start something with anyone, let alone a coworker. I admire your dedication to your job and appreciate your investment in this town, but that's where our relationship ends."

I dropped her hand as her smile shifted to a very irritated scowl. She gave a little huff and reached out to smooth a hand down her skirt. She cleared her throat and narrowed her eyes at me.

"You're a difficult man, Sheriff. I've never been one to back down from a challenge. I wouldn't be where I am today if I did."

It was on the tip of my tongue to tell her she didn't stand a chance, that I was already very interested in someone else, but that would inevitably lead to questions I wasn't ready to answer. Fortunately, the night deputy in charge of dispatch walked by my office at that exact moment. He stuck his head inside, shifting his gaze between me and the dark-haired woman who was still uncomfortably close.

"Sorry to interrupt. Got a call about an accident out on one of the farm roads. Sounds pretty serious. Sent some guys out and called the volunteer fire department already. Figured I should let you know since you're still in the office."

I breathed a sigh of relief and stepped around Delaney. "Thanks for letting me know. If it's serious, I better make sure the guys handle the scene appropriately." I reached for my hat, knocking loose papers and discarded coffee cups to the floor. I winced at the mess and mumbled, "I'll clean that up when I get back."

I was on my way out of the office door when a small hand latched on to my forearm. "You still haven't eaten, Rodie. You need to take better care of yourself. The *people* of this town need you."

It was easy to read between the lines. Sure, the town might need me, but it was obvious she thought she did as well.

"I'll grab something on my way out of town. You take care, Ms. Hall." I tipped the front of my hat and slipped out of her hold.

My deputy gave me a knowing look as I practically ran toward the front door of the small station.

"She sure is persistent." He sounded slightly envious.

I groaned. "She is. But I'm not interested." Would never be. She was as far from my type as anyone could be. Even when I'd been figuring things out and testing the limits of my sexuality, I'd never been drawn to small, dark-haired people. I much preferred the all-American, blond, blue-eyed look Wyatt Bryant was working with.

"She's pretty influential around these parts. Might not be in your best interest to play too hard to get." The other man called to my back as I pushed out the door. I didn't even stop and admonish him for speaking loudly enough for Delaney to hear.

Grumbling under my breath, I made my way to my SUV. This wasn't the first time in my life I'd been the object of unwanted advances, though it was the first time my continued rejections might affect my job and future in Sheridan. That pissed me off more than anything, to be honest. I'd already had to scramble to come up with a plan B for my entire life; I wasn't sure I had it in me to figure out a plan C.

I climbed behind the steering wheel, pausing and taking a deep breath when I realized the entire interior of the vehicle smelled like Wyatt's cologne. For some reason, the woodsy, fresh scent calmed down some of the turmoil churning under the surface of my outwardly calm demeanor.

Delaney Hall was absolutely not for me, but if I had anything to say about it, I was going to make Wyatt Bryant mine for as long as we could last without killing one another. I didn't have a clue what I was doing in my life outside of being a sheriff and being hung up on a pretty, wounded former special agent who was my polar opposite in almost every single way. Well, those two things didn't necessarily go together, but I was determined to find a way to make the two of us work.

CHAPTER 2

WYATT

I GROANED WHEN THE MORNING sun peeked through the decorative curtains on the wall of the bunkhouse. I'd been to the Warner ranch many times, for happy occasions and not so pleasant ones. This was the first time I'd been in one of the fancy, pricey bunkhouses they used for the guests who came to the property for a full, hands-on dude ranch experience. Families and adventurous types from all over the world made the trek to the ranch to experience the great outdoors and see what "roughing it" really meant. Never in a million years did I think Webb would find his place playing cowboy and tour guide for a living. However, he was calmer, more at peace, and far less dangerous now that he had a permanent place here on the massive property. My brother was great with people. He could charm even the hardest of hearts with minimal effort. He was also a natural when it came to handling the different animals on the ranch. He had a soft center hidden under his careless and carefree façade, and it was a relief to see him thriving, especially when I was so obviously not.

Webb and his girlfriend wanted me to stay with them when I agreed to come to Sheridan for a while. I'd eventually caved when Tennyson offered to move with Webb to DC to take care of me, even though she'd just taken a new job working with Rodie in the sheriff's office. I knew they would drop everything and show up on my doorstep if I didn't do something. I'd taken care of Webb our entire lives. I was the one who raised him. I was the one who protected him. We suffered and survived by relying on one another — and no one else. I knew it hurt him that I wouldn't let him hover over me while I adjusted to my new reality, and I'd told him until I had no more voice left to argue that he didn't need to return the favor. I was his big brother. It was my job to look out for him. I didn't take well to being treated like an invalid, and it was nearly impossible for me to ask for help, even when I needed it.

Swearing under my breath, I slowly rolled over onto my back, tossing my arm over my eyes and taking inventory of all the places my body throbbed and ached. It had been a mistake to act tough and pretend like I didn't need the cane in front of Webb yesterday. A combination of pride and stubbornness kept me from leaning on it while he guided me to the small, fully-stocked house I would call home until I figured out what I was going to do with my life. I didn't want him to know how slowly I was healing or how badly I was really hurting. I never wanted Webb to worry about me or feel like he'd somehow let me down by not being there when I nearly died. I didn't want him to spiral out of control when he thought about the fact it was his twin, our brother, who put me in this position. An out-of-control Webb was a very, very dangerous and unpredictable Webb.

So here I was, turning forty soon and relying on my baby brother for just about everything. Before I'd been gunned down in a devious plot orchestrated by Webb's twin, a twin we hadn't known about until recently, I figured I'd be happily settled down with a steady partner, planning a family, and advancing to a director position within the agency. None of those things had happened, even before the ambush.

My love life was practically nonexistent. It was hard to be with someone when I never knew where I was going to be sent or who I was going to have to pretend to be if I went undercover. My career was high risk, and it went without saying that because of my job, I was secretive by nature. Both those things made forming an honest and open connection with anyone very difficult. Since I'd pretty much proven that I couldn't keep a partner for longer than a month, family planning ended up being a pipe dream. I resigned myself to the fact I'd raised my baby brother, and he'd grown into a good man I was proud of. That would have to be enough of any fatherhood I'd ever get to experience. Yet, in the back of my mind, I'd always hoped for more.

As for work, I was good at my job. Passionate and dedicated. But sometimes the wheels of justice moved too slowly and I got impatient. I wasn't very good at toeing the line and had been my own worst enemy when it came to significant advancement. I was pretty sure the guys up the chain of command threw a party when I told them they could take their desk job and shove it. Not too many of my coworkers were sad to see me go, which was another heavy blow to my tattered pride.

I had no clue how I was supposed to find my next step, much less any sort of lasting relationship, in a place so far away from everything I'd ever known. But here I was. This detour was unplanned and honestly much harder to navigate than I expected.

I reached blindly for the bottle of painkillers next to the bed, popping one in my mouth and swallowing it dry. It took longer than I cared to admit to get myself out of bed and into the shower. My limbs felt like they were made out of cement, and my balance was shaky at best. I moaned the entire time I pulled on a pair of sweatpants. I considered making myself a pot of coffee and some breakfast, but honestly, it seemed too hard. All I wanted to do was lie back down on the soft bed and pull the covers over my head. I'd been doing that a lot lately.

Only, that was back in DC when I wouldn't have anyone nosy enough to come check up on me and make sure I was okay. I was in Sheridan now, and all hope of staying *undercover*, in a totally different way, *as in under the actual covers*, was shot to hell. Eventually, Webb was going to come see what I was up to, and for some reason that I couldn't explain, I refused to appear weak and vulnerable in front of my younger brother.

Almost as if I summoned the unwanted interruption with the power of my thoughts, a knock rattled the door of the bunkhouse. Assuming it was my brother, I limped over, pulled the door open, and turned back around without looking to see who was on the other side. Immediately, the scent of coffee and fresh-baked pastry hit my nose. My mouth started to water, but I when I turned to look, it wasn't Webb standing there holding breakfast.

"Cam?" I blinked down at the teenager who nervously shifted his weight from foot to foot. "Long time no see, kid."

Cameron Bauer was the teenage runaway the youngest of the Warner brothers had rescued from a horrific kidnapping. The teenager had almost ended up lost to a massive sex-trafficking ring. He was lucky he escaped by the skin of his teeth, and even luckier that the Warners had taken him in and claimed him as one of their own. The kid was sort of like a lost puppy, all wide-eyed and unsure of a life that included a loving family, a warm bed at night, and three square meals a day. Yet, oddly enough, even though he'd been living on the ranch longer than Webb, Cam still seemed skittish.

He held up the old-fashioned picnic basket and offered me a lopsided smile as I tugged the door open wide enough for him to enter the bunkhouse.

"Brynn made you breakfast. She was going to bring it down, but I wanted to see how you were doing. I heard you got hurt really bad on your last assignment." The teenager's eyes skimmed my bare torso, which was a patchwork of raised scars and puffy red skin that was still healing from multiple surgeries. He cringed as he shoved the basket into my hands. "Oh shit, it's worse than I expected."

I took the offering and set it on the obviously expensive, handcrafted kitchen table. I moved to pull a t-shirt on over my head in an attempt to hide my war wounds, and told Cam, "I'm okay."

I should've told him not to swear, but I couldn't do it. This kid had seen the worst humanity had to offer and had come out on the other side. A bad word here or there wasn't going to hurt him any more than the damage that his past had already inflicted.

"Does it still hurt? It looks like it hurts." Cam moved around the table and started pulling things out of the full basket.

Brynn Warner kept the ranch running like a well-oiled machine. She'd been taking care of the family and the patrons of the ranch since she was practically a child. Her history with the Warners was long and complicated, but now she was engaged to the youngest of the brothers. It was no longer a sore topic as to why she already had the same last name as the family. She'd earned her Warner status, and she was the best mother figure a kid like Cam could ask for. No one had a bigger heart than she did. And no one was a better cook, based on the smells emanating from the picnic basket.

"It hurts less than it did a week ago. I'm healing… slowly." I picked up a homemade cinnamon roll and sighed at how good it smelled. Thank God for Brynn, because there was no way I had the energy to look for food, much less prepare anything, and here she was saving the day again. "How you been, kid? Things good with you?"

I knew from Webb that Cam had recently started school in Sheridan. As someone who grew up on my own on the run, I knew how challenging it could be to finally settle into a normal routine. Add in that Cam had neon orange hair, a seriously prickly attitude, a fashion sense that you definitely didn't see out in the country, and the fact he was openly, proudly homosexual, I doubted his adjustment to typical teenage life had gone smoothly.

Cam offered up a shrug. "Things are okay."

I motioned to the basket and told him, "Help yourself." When he rummaged around inside, I asked him about his older brother. "How's Mikey doing?"

The Bauer brothers weren't as close as Webb and I. In fact, Cam's older brother was kind of a shithead who'd let the kid down time and time again. Although, he'd been horrified when he realized the lengths his younger sibling had gone to in order to survive on the streets, and his attitude changed slightly.

Cam shrugged again. "Doing all right. He's come up to visit a few times on break, but he's mostly focused on staying in school and his usual partying."

I snorted as I made myself a cup of coffee. I inhaled deeply and sipped slowly as I felt some of the sleepy fog dissipate thanks to the influx of caffeine and food in my system. "Sounds about right. How about you? Are you doing okay in school? Make any friends?"

Cam gave me a you've-got-to-be-kidding-me look as he plopped down in one of the seats tucked underneath the table. "Not really. I don't have anything in common with the kids at my school. Some of the girls are pretty nice. I think they like the novelty of having a gay BFF. They ask me for makeup and fashion advice, like I know anything about either of those things. The guys all avoid me or treat me like I'm some kind of alien." He rolled his eyes and gave me a shy glance under his eyelashes. "I still keep in touch with Ethan, though. We talk pretty much every day."

"Ahhh... I see." I hid my grin behind the rim of my coffee mug. Ethan was my former partner's stepson. Grady moved to New York with his new family not long after the mission that brought us both to Wyoming. I didn't know much about Grady's step kids, but he'd never mentioned that Ethan was gay, so I hoped Cam wasn't setting himself up for heartbreak. The kid deserved a break after all he'd been through. "Ethan's a good kid. I'm glad you have someone you can talk to, a friend you can trust. That's important."

"He's coming to visit this summer." The soft, dreamy expression that crossed his face did something to my heart. I knew that look. Every teenager who ever had a crush knew that look and what it felt like.

I remembered those feelings of first love. It was so delicate, so fragile. Mine had been shattered into a million pieces before it even had a chance to start. But the fact that Cam could still find it in himself to feel that way about someone after how terribly he'd been mistreated, well, it was honestly inspiring.

"That'll be fun."

He nodded and lifted his eyebrows at me. "The whole family is coming. If you're still around, you'll get to see Grady."

I huffed. "Grady came to DC after I got out of the hospital and helped me out. I wasn't exactly nice to him while I was laid up. I'm sure he's had enough of me and my rudeness to last a lifetime." My former partner was my best friend in the entire world. If Ethan was indeed attracted to Cam, the boys couldn't ask for a better advocate. He would have the boys' backs no matter what.

Cam grinned, but his expression quickly turned more serious. "Hey, I know you might not want to hear it, but I'm sorry about what happened to your brother and mom. Webb was really quiet about everything when he got back to the ranch, so I know losing them had to be difficult for you guys, even if you won't admit it." He lifted a hand and rubbed the center of his chest. "It sucked when my family cut me off, even though they were terrible people. It still hurts like a bitch."

I bit back a few dirty words and set my mug down on the table with more force than necessary. "Webb has a soft heart. Everything that happened was harder for him than it was for me. I'm okay, kid, don't worry about me. Anyway, don't you have to get ready for school?"

Webb's twin killed our mother, and attempted to kill Ten, just to leave Webb alone and lost in the world, the same way he'd been. Only, he didn't know Webb fell in love with a total badass, a woman who could hold her own in almost any situation, one who was armed and not afraid to pull the trigger. Ten killed Webb's twin, and we'd buried him and our mother on our family's land deep in the swamps of Louisiana. I was still physically healing during all of it, so a lot of the aftermath was a blur, thankfully. I could honestly say I hadn't grieved for either of them. It was probably a bad attitude to have, but my mother made my life a living hell and did her best to ruin me and my brother. I wasn't sad to have her permanently out of my life, and my long-lost brother nearly got me killed, so why was I supposed to be sorry that he ultimately got exactly what he dished out? It was a stretch for me to feel anything but indifference toward either of them.

Cam pushed away from the table, pausing to slap a hand on my shoulder. "You keep saying you're okay, Wyatt. Are you trying to convince me or yourself?" The teen gave my shoulder a squeeze and moved toward the door. "For whatever it's worth, I'm glad you're here. I really look up to you, and I know Webb is stoked he can keep an eye on you. He worries about you more than anyone." A sad smile pulled at his mouth. "You're lucky you have someone who cares about you like that."

He shot an absent wave in my direction as he disappeared out the door.

I wanted to tell him that he and Webb had more in common than he thought. I'd done my best to protect my brother, tried to keep him out of trouble and off the streets, but there were times in our past when we had to do some pretty questionable things. Even if Cam's older brother hadn't been a selfish little prick, there was no guarantee he would have been able to protect the kid from all the evil in the world.

Shaking my head to clear away the dark thoughts, I finished my coffee and tucked into another pastry. I was going to have to make my way up to the house so I could thank Brynn and say hello to the rest of the family. As slow as I was moving, however, it would take a while to get there, but I had to show my gratitude. They really were one-of-a-kind. There was no reason for them to take in another wounded stray, but they had done so without question. I was going to have to swallow my pride and pull out my cane. There was no way in hell I was covering that distance without something to lean on without ending up on my face in the dirt. I was also going to have to come clean with Webb about my current condition. He was going to see the cane and know I was the walking wounded.

I tried to convince him I was invincible, but the truth was, I broken just like everyone else.

I dragged myself to the shower, slowly and painfully stripping and climbing under the hot water. I waited to feel invigorated. Waited for some kind of spark, some kind of life to wake up inside of me. I'd been waiting since I turned in my badge and gun. I was a man used to having a purpose. I thrived under extreme conditions and was used to thinking on my feet. My mind hadn't quite adjusted to the limitations of my body, a situation that was entirely frustrating.

Fortunately, there was one part of my anatomy that still worked the way it always had. Even with the painkillers making my movements sluggish and slower than normal, my cock had no problem perking up under the water and reminding me exactly how long it'd been since it had some company.

Groaning, I wrapped a hand around the stiff length and let my mind wander. It shouldn't be a surprise that it immediately went to the surly sheriff of Sheridan. I'd been trapped in the car alone with him for hours yesterday. I could still hear the low rumble of his voice when we argued about everything. The touch of his thumb against my lip was seared into my memory. I could clearly see the way his jade eyes seemed to look right through me, and I had no trouble picturing the way his muscles flexed underneath his uniform. He was hot... so hot. I'd never really gone for the rugged and rough type, mostly because there weren't a ton of men who fit that bill in DC. It was a lot of suits and expensive styled hair. It was a lot of men looking to claw their way up different political ladders, which was exhausting when I was battling with them and doing the same thing myself.

So, not for the first time, and far from the last, I rested my forehead against the tiles and jerked myself off thinking about a guy I had no business getting worked up over. My life was enough of a mess as it was. The last thing I needed was to lust after a man who would run for the hills if he knew how often I pictured him naked.

CHAPTER 3

RODIE

"**B**OSS, JUST GOT A call from the high school. They're requesting you make an appearance."

I looked down at the radio with a frown and asked, "Why do I need to go? There's a patrol officer responsible for anything that happens at the school."

The deputy in charge of dispatch sighed and I could almost see the eye roll that accompanied the sound. "You have to go because the mayor's kid is involved, and he's the one requesting your presence on the scene."

"Fuck." The word slipped out before I could censor myself. I heard the deputy chuckle as I reached up to rub my forehead in aggravation. I was not the mayor's personal police dog. It annoyed me to no end that the man thought he could whistle and I'd come running obediently.

"What kind of dust-up are we talking about?" I better not be sacrificing my entire afternoon for something the administration at the school could handle in their sleep.

Another sigh blasted through the radio. "Mayor's kid got into it with a classmate. The new kid. The one Lane took in, so you know the entire Warner family is going to be up in arms. Mayor's kid is saying the new kid started it. The new kid is saying the mayor's boy attacked him unprovoked. Mayor's kid took the brunt of the fight and has a history of being problematic, according to the principal. I think the mayor wants you there as backup. Everyone in town knows he likes to throw his title around. But he's scared shitless of the Warners."

As he should be.

When the family banded together, they were basically unstoppable. I'd learned that lesson the hard way when I'd been forced into a corner and had to arrest Sutton, the middle brother, for murder. The rest of the Warners turned the town upside down until his name was cleared, and they'd never looked at me the same. They were a fearsome enemy to have, and the mayor knew it. The last thing I wanted to do was wade into the middle of this brewing storm, but it sounded like I didn't have much choice.

"All right. I'm headed that way. I'll report in once I'm free." The deputy wished me luck under his breath, and it was my turn to sigh. I smacked the palm of my hand on the steering wheel and whipped the SUV around to head to the high school. I hated the days when my job was more about playing politics than it was about keeping the town safe. I wasn't the most pragmatic and even-tempered man on my best days. My patience was limited when it came to smiling and shaking hands. I was pretty terrible at playing nice. But, I needed this job. It was the only thing tethering me to a sense of normalcy. It was the only thing that gave me a purpose and a reason to get up in the morning.

I grumbled dirty words under my breath as I marched into the school, which hadn't changed much since I'd attended. I went way back with the Warners. I remembered when Cyrus Warner, the eldest of the brothers, wanted out of Wyoming almost as badly as I did. We both swore we'd never come back. We had big dreams outside of Sheridan. Cy's dreams were cut short when he had to come back and take care of his family and their failing ranch. Mine literally blew up in my face. No matter how big and tough we were, or how much of the world we'd seen, and how we'd changed as we grew, we ended up back where we started when it was time to lick our wounds and regroup.

I could hear the mayor's booming voice as soon as I pushed through the main doors of the building. The entitlement and perceived authority in every word he snapped out made me cringe. I could hear the principal trying to placate the man and keep the situation calm.

"I want this little punk arrested! Look at my son's face! How can you call yourself the principal of this school when you let someone attack my child like this in broad daylight? I won't stand for this." The man huffed, and I noticed he was bright red as soon as I walked into the room.

The mayor was a fairly short, stout man. He looked a little bit like Yosemite Sam with his droopy mustache and oversized cowboy hat. Plus, his blustery, boastful attitude was similar to the cartoon character. Several of my deputies and I often laughed about the resemblance. It was hard to take him seriously, and his son took after him in both looks and demeanor. The teenager was sitting with his arms crossed over his barrel chest, glaring out of twin black and blue eyes at the other teen in the room.

Cameron Bauer stood out without even trying. Last time I saw the kid, he'd been skinny, all big eyes and skittish actions. Now, he'd filled out some, and was obviously taller and in better shape than the mayor's kid. He had a shock of dyed orange hair that I was certain could be spotted from space, and he had on a pink, v-neck t-shirt, black skinny jeans, and a pair of sneakers that looked like they had paint splattered all over them. I was sure they cost more than my mortgage payment. The look was distinct and flashy, especially in these parts. The kid was definitely not making an effort to blend in. I kind of admired him for it, but I also knew he wasn't doing himself any favors if he wanted to make it through the school year as easily as possible.

"Oh good, Sheriff Collins is here. I want you to arrest this miscreant for assault." The mayor put his hand on his son's shoulder and squeezed, which made the teenager wince. "Look what he did to Dalton."

The mayor's son looked petulant as he pouted and muttered, "He started it."

I looked over in Cam's direction, noticing he seemed unscathed for the most part. He had an icepack resting on the back of one hand, but he wasn't sporting the bruises the way the mayor's son was.

I sighed and gave the mayor a hard look. "Why are you confronting Cam without his guardian present? Do you think that's a good idea? You shouldn't get to gang up on him just because your child is involved in the altercation and you're a city official." I lifted an eyebrow in the principal's direction. "Someone has called the Warners, correct?" I made sure my tone let him know there was only one answer I wanted to hear.

The principal shifted his weight nervously, and I could practically see the wheels turning in his head as he scrambled for an excuse to cover his ass.

"I called Lane as soon as they hauled me into the office. He should be here any minute." Cam's voice was surprisingly calm considering the way the other adults in the room were glaring at him. "I didn't trust anyone here to have my back. I'm used to covering it myself."

The principal openly winced at being called out by the street-smart teenager.

"Arrest him, Rodie. That's a direct order." I looked over at the mayor when he snapped the command in my direction.

"Doesn't work that way." I rubbed my hand across my chin and looked between the boys. "First, I don't take orders from you. Second, Dalton says Cam started it. Where is the proof? Every teenager on the planet is attached to their cell phone these days. I'd bet good money if I confiscate every phone in this school, I can put together a video of the entire altercation. You good with that, boys?"

Dalton balked at the suggestion, and Cam threw back his head and laughed. The principal puffed up his chest and held up his hand, "Now now, I don't think we have to go to such extreme lengths. I have faith that the boys will be honest with us. And we can always ask the other kids who were in the locker room what happened when the altercation took place. We don't need to disrupt the entire school over this."

I snorted. "We don't? Cam's new here. Dalton's been in school with the same kids since preschool. That is not a fair and unbiased pool of witnesses."

"Your job is to protect this town, not to stick up for one kid who obviously doesn't belong." The mayor's tone was getting sharper and more hostile. I could see that he was getting more and more worked up each time I intervened on Cam's behalf. "If you don't do something about this situation, I will." The threat absolutely rubbed me the wrong way.

"No one wants to share a locker room with a fa—" Dalton's words were cut off when his father slammed his hand over the kid's mouth, but the damage had already been done.

I felt my eyebrows shoot up and the hair on the back of my neck lift. I gave Dalton a very pointed look and asked in a voice I could barely keep civil, "You got a reason why Cam shouldn't be in the locker room?"

Dalton pulled his father's hand away from his mouth and climbed to his feet. I automatically moved in front of Cam as the other boy shook a finger in his direction. "We have to strip and shower in the locker room. No one wants to get naked in front of a perv like him. I know he was checking me out. It was disgusting. He's lucky I didn't kill him."

Cam let out a dry chuckle and muttered, "As if." I wasn't sure if he was talking about checking Dalton out, or about

Dalton nearly killing him, either way his sarcastic response had me biting back a grin. Cam kept his composure far better than I would have.

"Why don't you go ahead and collect those cell phones, Sheriff?" Every head in the room whipped around as the slick, east coast accent suddenly filled the room.

My eyes widened in surprise as Lane Warner *and* Wyatt came storming into the front office. Well, Lane stormed, Wyatt sort of shuffled, still moving like every part of his body hurt. But his eyes were ice cold and totally calculating as he assessed the situation.

"If there is any evidence that Dalton started the fight *because* Cameron is gay, well, that can be classified as a hate crime and he could be looking at federal charges." Ice cold as always, Wyatt's voice cut through the tension in the room like a knife. He wasn't speaking to anyone in particular, but he made his point.

The mayor's face turned nearly purple, and every vein in his neck looked like it was about to pop as he started to sputter in Wyatt's direction. "Who the hell are you? What do you have to do with any of this? Rodie, is this how you control a sensitive situation? I'm starting to question endorsing you to serve another term."

"You cornered Cam for questioning and made him face his accuser without his guardian present. Your son is spouting homophobic slurs and murder threats in front of the school's principal and law enforcement. There is little I can do to make this situation better for you, Mayor." I made the statement as blandly as possible, watching as the other man got worked up until he was nearly vibrating in his cheap suit. I hooked a thumb in Wyatt's direction and gave the flustered mayor a smirk. "And he's a former federal agent. If he says we can look at this as a hate crime, I believe him."

Lane immediately went to Cam, giving the teenager a onceover as he addressed the principal with a dangerous growl,

"My kid gets hurt and you didn't bother to call me? But you called the mayor? You're a fool if you think I'm going to let that pass without recourse."

The principal gulped and nervously fiddled with one of the buttons on his shirt. "I didn't know it was such a big deal. I thought we could handle it amongst ourselves. It's just boys being boys."

Lane snorted. He crossed his arms over his chest and glared at the other man until he actually flinched and looked away. "Only, one of the boys is new to the area and just so happens to be gay, and the other is the son of the town's mayor. If you think I can't see how you're trying to railroad Cam, you're as dumb as you look."

The principal let out a shaky breath and ran his hands through his hair. "What if I discipline both boys? They can take equal responsibility for what happened and we can keep the law out of it."

"No!" Dalton practically screamed the words out. "He doesn't belong here. He's a freak who doesn't know his place. He's weird and different. Nobody wants him here. I didn't do anything wrong."

I had to physically hold Lane back when he suddenly lunged forward. Lane was the most easygoing of the Warners, but it was obvious he couldn't keep his cool when his kid was threatened. While I had my hands full keeping Lane under control, Wyatt shuffled toward an indignant Dalton.

"Listen, kid, I know you don't come by that hate and ignorance on your own. That's something you learn young." Even though I couldn't see his expression, I was pretty sure he was looking at the mayor. "In this life, you're going to encounter a lot of different kinds of people. Some of those differences you might not agree with, but it isn't your job to police what is and what isn't normal for someone else. You might be a big fish in a small pond right now, but when you eventually swim out into the ocean, you're gonna find out just how tiny you, and that ugly mindset of yours, really are. Pick a fight with a shark, and you're gonna get eaten alive."

I had to give it to the kid, though. Cam had already proven he was no one's target and that he wouldn't be anyone's punching bag.

Lane growled again and bit out, "I want to press charges. I'm not letting that entitled brat get away with attacking Cam for no fucking reason."

The mayor started swearing. The principal started sweating bullets. Lane looked like he was ready to rip everyone in the room to shreds, but Wyatt stayed silent and calm as chaos swirled around us. I was supposed to be keeping the peace, but I found myself staring at him, captivated. I could see why he was so good at his previous job. You had to have ice in your veins when you went undercover, and Wyatt was practically frozen as he watched the mayor try to salvage a situation which was quickly deteriorating.

I put my fingers in my mouth and let out a shrill whistle, making everyone in the room go silent. I used a finger to tilt back the brim of my hat and addressed the entire room.

"Dalton should be suspended for instigating the fight and violating the school's zero-tolerance toward bullying policy. If you press charges, at most he's going to get community service. I'm going to suggest the school implement sensitivity training and awareness for all the students and staff instead. Wyatt is right. Wyoming isn't the center of the universe, and the kind of attitude Dalton has toward someone different is outdated and dangerous. I'm taking a formal complaint from Cam. If anything else happens to him while he's on school property, I'm sure the Warners will have no problem taking you to court for negligence and discrimination. It's your job to keep every student in this building safe while they get an education. Am I making myself crystal clear… to all parties?" I didn't want a temporary solution for Cam. I wanted to make his world safer for the long run. I hoped Lane would see that.

The principal nodded aggressively and looked somewhat relieved… until Lane barked, "Oh, I'm not waiting until something else happens. You don't get to haul my kid in during a situation like this without letting me know what's going on."

Feeling like my job was mostly done, and knowing that Lane was just getting started on ripping the school official a new one, I tried to slip out the door unnoticed.

No such luck.

The mayor grasped my forearm and hauled me around as soon as I reached the doorway. The short man glared up at me, face still flushed and fury evident in his gaze.

"I thought you would have my back in there. What exactly was that, *Sheriff?*"

I snorted and shook loose from his hold. "That was me mitigating the damage *your* son caused. Do you not know how lucky you are they aren't making this a federal case? Your son's future would be destroyed if he was convicted of a federal crime. You may want to take care of your own house first, *Mayor.*"

The man's eyes narrowed to thin slits as his mouth pressed into a tight, hard line. "I'd be very careful where you are treading, Rodie. Why are you defending a boy like that? It's almost like you have sympathy for *those* people. And if you do," he shook his head slightly, "I can't say you're the best fit for the position of sheriff any longer."

Those people.

I gritted my teeth, put my hand on the center of the man's chest, and pushed him out of my space.

"Thankfully, it's up to the people of Sheridan to decide that." It was on the tip of my tongue to tell the man I was one of *those* people, but I kept it in. "I'll take my chances that the job I've done over the last few years speaks for itself."

I left the room before I did something that I would regret. I nearly ran over Wyatt, who was waiting silently in the hallway as I made my exit.

He wobbled slightly from the collision and I had to put a hand on his arm to keep him upright. I was impressed by the flex of muscle under his shirt. He might look slightly breakable at the moment, but he still felt solid under my fingertips.

He shook off my hand and looked up at me with icy eyes. "Do you really think telling them to be nice and considerate of people's differences is going to make any difference? All you're doing is putting a spotlight on Cam and letting the instigator get away with his crime." He narrowed his eyes. "That kid has never had anyone advocate for him. You're going to be one more authority figure, one more adult, who has let him down."

I swore under my breath and returned the blond man's glare. "You and I both know the likelihood of federal charges being brought against him is slim to none. You have to know that any judge in this county who sees the mayor's kid in his courtroom is going to go easy on him. This is a small town. Things here don't work the way they do in DC, pretty boy. Now, everyone knows if they mess with Cam, there will be repercussions. Even the mayor's son can be expelled, but he has to learn about being sensitive to others. It's the best solution out of a handful of shitty options."

Wyatt made a noise and tilted his head back so he could glare up in my direction. "It's an option that lets you stay totally in the middle of the street. Just like when you arrested Sutton, even though you knew he did not hurt his child's mother. You always do what's expected, what minimizes any blowback in your direction. The mayor is an asshole, but he may be right that you're not the best person for the job of keeping the people— some who mean the world to me—safe."

He went to step back, but was unsteady and reached out for something to hold onto. Unfortunately for him, I was the closest thing for him to grab. His hand fisted in my shirt, pulling us chest to chest. My breath audibly caught and I watched Wyatt's eyes pop wide. The blue of his gaze was endless and as deep as the ocean. It was so cheesy and cliché, but I honestly could drown in those eyes.

I reached out and put a hand on Wyatt's hip, holding him until he was once again steady on his feet. His eyebrows shot upward and his fist tightened in the material of my shirt. I felt my pulse kick up and my breath hitch slightly. Wyatt frowned, but I saw the bright pink flush work its way up the long line of his neck.

We broke apart when the door behind us swung open. Cam came running out, immediately going to Wyatt, telling him how cool he'd been and how grateful he was that he'd come to his defense. The kid barely spared me a glance, but I didn't miss the way Lane scowled at me or the way the mayor took in how close I was standing to the tall blond man in front of me.

I liked my life in Sheridan. Things were typically predictable and easy. I never regretted coming back home when I had nowhere else to go. It was a life I fought for and worked my ass off to keep afloat. Any idiot could see things were about to get complicated, and I wasn't sure if I was ready for that. After all, it was my job to clean up messes, not make ones of my own.

But, even with unease brewing in the background, I knew I couldn't let whatever it was that woke up inside of me around Wyatt go back to sleep.

Because while I enjoyed my simple, easy life... I rarely felt *alive* the way I did when I was around him. It'd been a long time since anyone made me want to do more than go through the motions.

CHAPTER 4

WYATT

"YOU KNOW, WE'D LOVE to have you stay up at the actual house with us, Wyatt. You don't have to make that walk across the property every time you join us for dinner." Leo Warner flashed me a bright smile as she passed over a plate of barbecue ribs. The smell made my mouth water, but her words had me fighting back a flinch. I thought I was doing a pretty good job of hiding just how hard it was for me to get around.

Apparently, I wasn't that good of an actor. There was no disguising the way the effort to make it to the main house made me sweat and my healing muscles shake.

Leo was the newly minted matriarch of the Warner clan. She married Cyrus not too long ago. She'd come to Wyoming for a girls' getaway, which had gone horribly wrong. She'd ended up smack dab in the middle of the undercover assignment I was working on. There had been lots of blood and bullets in her and Cy's love story, meaning the former big city executive had more than earned her place next to the rugged ranch owner. Nowadays, Leo was the one who looked more like a lifelong Wyomingite in her boots, braids topped by a cowboy hat, and plaid shirts. Cy never really embraced western attire, and instead looked like he picked most of his outfits from the nearest motorcycle rally. Which was why Lane was the face of the business. The youngest Warner was everyone's idea of what a tall, sexy, capable cowboy should be. The picture of Lane on the website and the tourist brochures, with his dark hair, bright blue eyes, and guitar in hand, did more to draw women to the remote ranch than anything else. And he was completely okay being the eye candy poster boy for the Warner ranch if it meant he could continue doing what he loved.

After spooning some potato salad and baked beans on my plate, I met the redhead's probing gaze from across the massive wooden dining table.

"It's fine. The exercise is good for me. I was seeing a physical therapist in DC pretty regularly before I left. I guess slacking off has taken its toll." I was much stiffer and experiencing more pain than before I left. But, considering I was spending my days spinning my wheels and mourning what used to be, I had no one to blame for the backslide other than myself. I patted my very flat stomach and wiggled my eyebrows at Brynn Warner, who was seated next to me. "And I've finally managed to get back to my fighting weight. I haven't eaten this well..." I trailed off after a moment, realizing I'd *never* actually eaten this well. When we were kids, we practically starved on the regular. In the army, you ate when you got a chance, and it was never anything gourmet. In DC, I dined out often, sometimes on a date, but usually, I ate alone. Since coming to the Warner's ranch, I'd had three square meals a day, and I typically ate dinner with the entire clan at least twice a week. It was the first time in my life I'd experienced regular family dinners. "I've never eaten this well. You're an amazing chef and I can't tell you all how much I appreciate what you've done for me."

Cy snorted and lifted one of his salt and pepper eyebrows in my direction. There were not a lot of men in the world who intimidated me. I knew I could hold my own in pretty much any situation, and I had been in my fair share of life-threatening situations where I came out the victor. There was simply something about Cy, some kind of aura, that silently warned he was not a man you wanted to test. He was, however, a man you wanted on your side, and I was eternally grateful he'd taken Webb under his wing and became his mentor. All the ways in which Webb had changed for the better were directly related to Cyrus Warner seeing the value and potential in my brother. He was the only other person who'd taken the time to look besides me… and of course, Tennyson McKenna. My brother's pretty blonde girlfriend was watching the exchange silently, seeing more than I wanted her to, I was sure. She had a knack for reading people, and I was sure my general unease and frustration with my body was evident to her.

There was no keeping secrets at this table. They were all too perceptive and cared too much about me.

"Not doing it for you, Wyatt. We're doing it for us. We've all been worried sick about you, knowing you were hurt and handling everything on your own. That's not how we do things in this family." Cy's silver eyes cut deep into me, saying more than his words did.

I cleared my throat and let out a small smile. It'd been a long time since I'd felt like part of a family. It'd always been me and Webb against the world, but even so, I'd had to leave him behind when I enlisted, so as usual, I ended up on my own. It was slightly overwhelming to have the Warners embrace me as one of their own.

"I didn't mean to make anyone worry. I just had a lot to deal with when I decided to leave my job. I've always dealt with unpredictability in my career. I didn't realize how difficult it was going to be when all of that uncertainty went away, and each day looked like the one before it. I may have sulked a little longer than was healthy." Not to mention I had my mother's death and all the chaos created by Webb's truly evil twin to deal with while I was practically bedridden. In my mind, I'd earned the months-long pity party I threw for myself.

"There's a really good physical therapist in Sheridan." Ten piped up from her place next to Webb. She pointed the end of her fork in my direction. "I can get her info next time I'm in town." The statuesque woman looked like she should've been a supermodel, but in actuality, she was a former FBI agent and one of the best trackers on the planet. It seemed like there wasn't anyone she couldn't find, so it was no surprise Rodie put her in charge of the entire county's search and rescue team when she went to work for him. She kept busy, and I was jealous. I would've loved to have a job custom-made for me fall in my lap any day now, something to give me a purpose since I was just floundering.

I nodded to show I was agreeable to taking the information. Turning my head, I looked over at Cam who was seated next to me. His brightly dyed head was bent down, and his gaze was locked on his phone. It was so very *teenager*, and the normalcy of it made me smile. Cam should be focused on his phone and his friends while ignoring the adults at family dinner. It was the most basic of interactions, but one he'd been denied. Cam's parents were devoutly religious, so much so, they couldn't see the special, wonderful child they'd been blessed with beyond his sexual orientation. Cam's father honestly believed he could 'pray the gay away.' And when that hadn't worked, he beat his son and terrorized him, all in the name of his beliefs. Eventually, Cam left. He was barely a teenager and had no clue how the big bad world worked. Immediately, the streets ate the poor kid up and spat him out. That he was here now, surrounded by people who loved and appreciated him, and acting like all the horrors of his past hadn't left indelible scars, was pretty miraculous.

I nudged him with my elbow, forcing him to look up at me. The gleam in his dark eyes, and the tell-tale pink in his cheeks indicated he was probably talking to Ethan instead of eating his dinner.

"How have things been at school?" I worried about him, but Lane insisted things were going fine after the fight and intervention.

Cam lifted a shoulder and let it fall. He pushed some of his orange hair out of his face and gave me a lopsided grin. "It's okay. Lane scared the crap out of the principal, and all the teachers seem like they're being extra watchful." He smirked at me. "Dalton had no clue that I knew how to fight. He figured since I like boys, I'd be an easy target. He had no idea I used to fight for my life on a regular basis. Most of his crew leave me alone now." He cocked his head a little and gave me a questioning look. "Plus, Sheriff Collins has come by the school a few times to check on me. He's a pretty scary dude. Anyone who wanted to give me shit thought twice about it since he's keeping an eye on me."

Brynn made a noise and told Cam, "Don't swear at the dinner table."

It was such a *mom* thing to say. It came naturally to her, and it made me smile. Cam immediately apologized and did his best to look sheepish.

Deciding to rescue the kid, I asked, "Rodie's been checking up on the school?" It didn't really fit with my image of the taciturn sheriff.

"Rodie's not a bad guy." Cy's deep voice cut into our quiet conversation. "When he was young, he had a hard time fitting in here. When he came back, he'd changed, and ever since he became sheriff, I think he's caught between the expectations of the town and doing what he knows is best for everyone."

Lane snorted. "Well, let's not sing those praises too loudly, shall we? Did you forget he arrested Sutton for murder?"

That was a sore spot the family still hadn't gotten over.

Ten sighed and now pointed her fork at the dark-haired Warner. "The evidence pointed to Sutton. We all know he couldn't have done it, wouldn't have done it, but there was evidence, and Rodie had to do his job." She dropped the fork on her plate and shrugged. "If I'd been in his shoes, I probably would've arrested Sutton, too." Her green eyes cut in my direction. "What about you, Wyatt? If the evidence is compelling, would you make an arrest even if you personally knew the suspect and doubted their involvement?"

I paused before I answered. That was a tricky question, and I wasn't sure if my personal history would keep me unbiased if I were in the same situation. Webb didn't exactly have a perfectly clean criminal record, but I knew my little brother's hard limits. He was capable of some bad stuff, but he wasn't the kind of man who could commit murder. So, I wasn't sure if I could blindly follow procedure if I were in the same position as Rodie had been.

"Doesn't matter. Rodie changed the way folks in town looked at Sutton, so he left." Lane dropped his fork on his plate with a clatter and glared at Ten. "The sheriff's a dick."

"Hey!" Brynn kicked the dark-haired cowboy under the table as she jerked her head in Cam's direction. "Behave."

"Sutton didn't leave because of Rodie." Cy's deep voice was unwaveringly calm and even. "He left because he didn't want to be reminded of his daughter's kidnapping and the fact that a madman nearly killed the woman he loved right in front of him every time he stepped out the front door."

The middle Warner brother was working on an equine therapy ranch out in Northern California. He'd taken his daughter and Leo's best friend, Emrys, with him. The couple were now parents to two adorable children and seemed to be thriving on the West Coast. Clearly the youngest Warner had yet to come to terms with the change in the family dynamic.

"I don't know the sheriff very well. But he does seem committed to his job, and I don't think he would've moved on your brother if he didn't have some really, really compelling evidence. I think he was caught between a rock and a hard place. I'm honestly impressed he actually pulled Sutton in. You guys are scary one on one, going up against all of you," I shook my head and smiled. "He's gotta have brass balls."

I snapped my mouth shut and ordered my mind away from Rodie's balls, visualizing Rodie's balls, and wanting to do really amazing things to Rodie's balls. That was seriously dangerous territory, and not at all appropriate for dinner.

Seeing the need for a change in subject, Leo jumped to the rescue, looking between me and Webb with bright, inquisitive eyes. "How long are you planning on staying, Wyatt? Webb said you sold your condo in DC, and I assume you have no interest in going back to Louisiana. Do you think you're going to settle down here in Wyoming?" Her smile was sincere when she said, "We'd all love to have you close by."

I shrugged my good shoulder. I was going for nonchalant, but wasn't sure I pulled it off. "I don't have any set plans. Once I get back to my old self, I have to figure out what I'm going to do for a living. I can't be an indefinite guest here." I refused to overstay my welcome.

My brother snorted and turned his head so he could glare at me from down the table. "You don't need to work. I told you, you can have every cent that bastard left to us. Go live a life of leisure. Travel the world. Find a good man and settle down. Adopt a hundred babies who need a good home. There are plenty of options for you, Wyatt. You just refuse to consider any of them."

When we'd gone hunting for Webb's twin, we'd inadvertently run across our father. The man wanted nothing to do with us, but he had set up trust funds in our names to pay for college and other miscellaneous needs. Our mother never told us about the money, so it sat and accrued interest for years. Between Webb's and his twin's amount, along with my own, it was a significant chunk of money. A life-changing amount. Only neither Webb nor I wanted to touch it.

It felt dirty.

It felt like blood money.

Sighing, I pushed my mostly cleared plate away and glared at my brother. "I'm not a life of leisure kind of guy, but I will figure something out. I always do." I moved away from the table, shaking my head when Brynn immediately rose and told me she would get me dessert to take down to the bunkhouse. Having so many people hovering over me was kind of nice, but I was used to doing my own thing and calling my own shots without answering to anyone. All this consideration could become suffocating if I wasn't careful.

I shuffled to the front door, grabbing the cane I'd left resting on the porch. There was no use hiding it from Webb anymore. He was watching me too closely, and I couldn't get across the property without it, especially in the fading light.

I made my way slowly to the bunkhouse, enjoying the changing colors of the sky. The Wyoming sky was like a massive watercolor painting. The vivid colors blended so beautifully. It seemed so huge without lights or city pollution hampering the view. I could see why so many people came here to escape and to heal. There was something about the vastness and silence of it all that was soothing to the soul.

I hauled my tired body into the shower, spent more time having illicit fantasies about a certain someone, and passed out satisfied but empty on the inside. Webb wanted me to have a plan, but I honestly didn't know what my next move should be. I was used to being on the go and living out of a suitcase. Pretending to be someone new with every job assignment. Waking up to the same ceiling, and having the same people concerned about my well-being day in and day out was an entirely new concept. Being myself everyday was an experience that I hadn't had to think about in so long. I'd always wanted to put down roots and have a family, but now I wondered if the normalcy of it all was too constrictive for a guy who really had no clue how a family worked.

I'd been practically feral my entire life. I wasn't sure if I was the type to be domesticated, even though I convinced myself that was my dream.

I passed out with the troubled thoughts still swirling and spent the night tossing and turning. Needless to say, I wasn't thrilled when someone pounded on my door what felt like mere hours later. I squinted against the sun and crawled out of bed. Figuring it was probably Cam dropping off an early breakfast again, as had become his custom, I pulled on a pair of sweats to cover my nakedness and made my way to the door.

I pulled it open, absently scratching a hand across my chest. "I told you, you don't have to come all the way down here before school. I'm a grownup. I can find food on my own." I muttered the words as I shuffled across the floor.

"You most definitely are all grown up. Have to say, I'm pretty fond of that fact, Special Agent."

I felt my eyes pop wide and my hand latched onto the edge of the door so I didn't fall backward. The shock of his voice made me unable to get my bearings.

The last person I expected to see on my doorstep was Rodie Collins. And I sure as hell never would have expected him to be so blatantly checking me out. There was no missing the way his gaze lingered on the front of the sweats, where the thin, worn fabric was leaving very little to even my imagination.

I felt myself blush as I fought the urge to cover my naked chest with my arms like some Victorian virgin. I didn't like the way Rodie seemed to see right through me. But I did like the way his gaze almost felt like a physical touch. It'd been a long time since my skin had felt that heated tingle of arousal, especially from just a glance.

"What are you doing here, Sheriff?"

I grunted as Rodie rudely pushed his way around me and walked into the small space. He was careful when he put his hands on me. He made me move, but he also made sure I didn't go flying or fall over at the sudden shift in weight.

"I was hoping for coffee, but it looks like I woke you up." His eyes flicked over me once again, and he waved a hand in my direction. "Wash up and get dressed. I'll put a pot on while I wait."

I huffed and slammed the door shut. "What do you want, Rodie?" He always knew how to push my buttons. I needed to get better at hiding my reactions to him.

"Ten called last night and told me you need to get back on a physical therapy regimen. There's only one person in town who can deal with your kind of injuries and has the experience you need. She's a friend of a friend; I'm taking you to see her. This is the only time she's available, so get a move on, pretty boy."

I froze, mouth dropping open in shock. "Excuse me?"

Rodie didn't bother to turn from where he was messing with the coffee maker. "Hurry up, Wyatt. She's the best you're gonna get out in these parts. Don't be stupid and let your pride convince you there are better options."

I shook my head dumbfounded. "No, why are you involved? Why is Ten talking about me with you?" I was confused and right on the edge of being pissed off. I loved my brother's girlfriend a lot. I admired and respected her, but she sent Rodie to get me from the airport, and now this. It felt like she was greatly overstepping her boundaries.

Rodie turned around and lifted his eyebrows when he saw I had yet to move. "She told me because I asked. I'm curious about you... I worry about you."

A shiver raced up my spine and I felt my hands curl into tight fists at my sides. "Why?"

A smile that literally stole the breath from my lungs and made my already shaky knees turn liquid crossed the other man's distractingly handsome face.

"Figure it out for yourself, Special Agent." He picked up a coffee mug and gave me a smirk. "Go get dressed, or I'll haul you into town the way you are."

I blinked and suddenly bolted — well, awkwardly limped — toward the bathroom. I closed the door and flipped the lock with trembling fingers.

What in the hell was that?

There was no way he meant what I thought he meant... was there?

CHAPTER 5

RODIE

"HOW DO YOU KNOW this physical therapist? You said she's a friend of a friend, but I have a hard time picturing you having many friends." Wyatt's tone was dry and snide, but he was fidgeting nervously in the passenger's seat of my SUV. I wasn't sure if the nervous energy was coming from the trip into town to see the PT, or because he caught me checking him out when he answered the door half-naked.

I didn't bother to hide my overt interest in him, and I expected questions. Instead, Wyatt went almost shy, hurrying to cover up a body that, while was still clearly defined and in great shape, had obviously seen better days. Seeing the wounds and the patchwork of red, raised lines from the incisions of multiple surgeries gave me flashbacks to my own long, painful road to recovery. I hated that for Wyatt, and hated the way he seemed embarrassed to be sporting so many battle wounds. I wasn't wrong when I told him that being here at all was a beautiful thing, especially now that I could see how close he'd come to leaving this Earth.

"I've been tight with Ten and Sutton since high school." When you befriended one Warner, the others followed naturally. "They were the only kids who didn't make fun of me for being the poor kid with a young mom. They didn't care about the fact I didn't really fit in, and they were the only kids who really understood why I wanted out of Sheridan." I looked at Wyatt out of the corner of my eye, noticing that he was processing each word I said. The guy was a great investigator, and I was sure he could read between the lines of what I was saying. He wasn't the only one with a screwed-up family and a whole lot of very heavy baggage.

"I have a few buddies from the Marine Corps I keep in touch with, but you're right, I'm not necessarily close to anyone. This job makes it hard to maintain impartial friendships." And when personal and professional lines crossed, it never ended well. Arresting Sutton Warner for murder was a prime example of that. "However, I had a commanding officer when I was a new recruit in the military who sort of took me under his wing when I was struggling in boot camp. He was a good man, kept me out of trouble and turned me into a highly skilled soldier. He was and still is the man I look up to most in my life. When he retired, he moved to Sheridan and bought a little piece of property and some cattle. I guess he always wanted to be a cowboy, and after so many years running black ops missions and watching people die, he was ready for space, peace, and quiet. Being around good men doing bad things for the safety of their country takes its toll. Miranda, the physical therapist you're going to see, is his widow. She moved up here with him and set up shop. She's also a former Marine and one of the best at rehabbing the kind of traumatic injuries you have. She'd make a fortune if she moved to a bigger city, but she stays here because it reminds her of the man she loved. They were both happy here."

Wyatt shifted in the seat, and I could practically hear the gears turning in his complicated mind. "If you were so ready to leave, why did you come back? I know Cyrus had to come home when his dad got sick, and Ten came home when things went south with her job and her relationship, but what about you? You don't strike me as the type to run home when the going gets tough."

Interestingly enough, his acknowledgement was a compliment, even if it didn't sound like one. I turned my head slightly so I could grin at the blond man sulking next to me. I winged up an eyebrow and told him, "I ended up back here for the same reason you did. I got hurt and needed someone to take care of me. I didn't have anyone other than my former CO willing to step up and help out. He was the closest thing I had to family, and the only person who understood how lost and alone I felt when I was told I would no longer be a soldier. I'd lost everything important to me back then, and Sheridan was the place that gave me my purpose back, made my life worth living again."

Wyatt's head whipped around and his bright blue eyes widened. His mouth moved, but no words came out as our similar stories settled heavily in the space separating us. After a moment, he shook his head as if to clear it and those columbine eyes narrowed slightly. "What happened to you? How bad was it that they discharged you without a fight?"

The military invested a lot of time and money training their elite soldiers. He would know that, being one himself. He wasn't wrong that, under different circumstances, they wouldn't have let me go so easily, but considering I was barely breathing and only had a fifteen-percent chance of a full recovery, the powers that be couldn't show my ass to the door fast enough.

"I was blown up." The words used to hurt when I said them. They used to bring on weeks of nightmares and would cause me to break out in a cold, full-body sweat. I still didn't talk about the incident lightly, but my mind had healed along with my body over the years. Just like Wyatt's would. He just needed time, and someone to help him deal with the feelings of not having a purpose or a reason to get up each day. Part of me thought that I could be his salvation, if he'd let me.

I heard him draw in a sharp breath, and he suddenly seemed more alert in the seat next to me. "Blown up? Did you roll over an IED?"

It was always nice to have this kind of conversation with a fellow military man. There was an inherent understanding there. It was easier when I was explaining the circumstances to someone who could actually picture the dangerous circumstances most people couldn't even dream of.

I shook my head and tapped my fingers on the steering wheel, doing my best to stay focused on the road and not let myself get sucked into old memories and nightmares that once haunted me on the regular.

"No. My unit was on a rescue mission in Kandahar. Went in to pull out a couple of British reporters who were taken captive. Intel was bad. The building was wired to blow as soon as we breached the perimeter. I was the team leader, so you know, first guy in. Had nearly the entire structure come down on top of me. I don't remember much after the first explosion. I woke up in Germany almost three weeks later. My pelvis was shattered. Both my arms were broken. I had all kinds of memory issues and none of the doctors thought I was ever going to walk again." I blew out a breath and tightened my hands on the steering wheel. "I was actually lucky. The journalists were dead before we were even on the scene, and the unit sent in to pull us out of the wreckage was ambushed. None of them made it. So, yeah, I was the lucky bastard in that scenario."

The guilt I felt whenever relaying that part of the story was thick and heavy. I always felt like I was going to choke on the memory and the words felt like they were lodged in my throat.

Wyatt sighed and tossed his head back against the seat. He closed his eyes and I noticed that his hands curled into fists where they were resting on top of his thighs. "No one is lucky when it comes to war. Even the guys who come home without obvious injury still carry what they've seen. I enlisted because it was the only way I could think of to save my brother and keep us both off the street. I was sure whatever the army asked me to do would be easier than what living on the streets forced me to do. I was wrong." He tilted his head in my direction and opened one eye. "You seem okay now. Your CO and his old lady took good care of you, it looks like."

I shrugged a little and turned my eyes back to the road. "They didn't let up on me until I could walk on my own. It was grueling, but I was honestly more worried about what I was going to do with my future. All I knew was being a Marine. There weren't many options out there for me. It was my CO's idea that I should run for sheriff. My history with this town isn't exactly all roses and rainbows, so I thought he was out of his mind to suggest it."

I was also reluctant because I was tired of being two different men. One wore a uniform and lived his life by the standards of others, and one felt confined and bitter that he was never able to be free to love who he wanted to love. Both of those men ended up isolated and lonely, but eventually, my fear for my future put me in a place where running for sheriff seemed like my only option. Plus, I had my CO and Miranda in my corner, so I didn't feel as alone. I'd had them both until my former CO succumbed to demons I didn't even know he was fighting and took his own life. Wyatt was right; sometimes the invisible wounds from war ran deeper and were far more damaging than the ones on the surface.

"The town must have a short memory. You've been re-elected every time you've run for the position." There was a hint of begrudging respect in Wyatt's tone.

I dropped a shoulder in a loose shrug. "The first time I ran, the old sheriff was getting ready to retire and the other guy running got a DUI right before the election and was forced to drop out. It was a close call. I feel like I've done my best for the people and proven myself over the years, so they've continued to pick me, even when there was a worthy opponent."

"The mayor mentioned there's an election around the corner. Are you running unopposed this term, as well?" It was small talk, but I couldn't help the little burst of satisfaction that he was finally showing some interest in me and my life.

"So far. But the mayor was pretty upset with the way I handled things at the high school. He's called the office every single day to let me know he's on the lookout for a viable candidate to replace me." I'd blown him off, but I knew the threat was real. The man didn't like being ignored and publicly embarrassed, and he very well could make the next election a fight if he felt like I wasn't willing to pander to his every whim.

"That guy is an idiot, and he's raising a hateful bully. That kid is going to get out in the real world and be shocked that his way of thinking is frowned upon and laughed at."

"True, or he's going to stay close to home and turn into an even bigger bully with his dad's title to back him up. It's a lot harder to leave here than it seems." And it was much harder to stay away than I ever believed.

Wyatt made a noise low in his throat and closed his eyes again. "Cam's a tough kid. He deserves to have a normal childhood. That mayor and his kid are in for a hard road ahead if they think they're going to go up against the Warners and win. I've never met a family as tight and determined. They'll be a wall surrounding Cam and no one is getting through. That family will go to the mat for someone they love every damn time."

I nodded even though he couldn't see what I was doing. "I know that." I was actually envious. I wondered how different my life would've been if I'd had anyone like the Warners in my corner when I was a scared teenager who struggled with the fact that I wasn't like the other boys my age. I'd never had anyone blindly accept me in my life, and I was glad Cam had landed in a place surrounded by champions and heroes.

Almost as if he'd read my mind, Wyatt muttered, "I wish I'd had someone on my side like that when I was his age. When I was little, we lived in the deep south, and being gay was not something we talked about or even acknowledged, even well before I knew I was gay. When I got older and refused to pretend to be someone I wasn't, it made an already tough situation with my mother virtually impossible. She told me the reason she was leaving me and Webb was because I was a disgrace who went against God. The woman abused us. Starved us. Abandoned us. Manipulated us. And yet, *I* was the one who was broken and wrong." His eyes popped open and his mouth pulled into a fierce frown. He so rarely smiled, I wondered if he even remembered how. "I used to stay up all night long wondering and worrying about what Webb would say when he got old enough to realize I was gay. I made myself sick too many times to count thinking he would leave me, too. He never cared one way or the other, but my sexuality definitely didn't make his life any easier when we were growing up. I would have given anything to have just one Warner in my corner back in those days."

I started a little, head whipping around as I pulled to a stop at one of the few lights leading into Sheridan. It was the first time Wyatt had outright said he was gay to me. I knew it wasn't something he went out of his way to hide, but it also wasn't a topic of conversation he tossed around freely. How different we were in that regard. I respected and was even a bit envious of his freedom.

While we were stopped, Wyatt turned to look at me, questions bright and sharp in his gaze. "Why did you ask Ten about me? Why did you pull strings with your friend to get me in for a consultation? We aren't friends. We hardly know each other. I can't figure out your angle, Sheriff. Whatever it is, I don't like it."

Pulling forward I muttered, "I've told you that we have more in common than you think, Special Agent. I understand pretty much every single struggle you've been through on a soul-deep level." I arched an eyebrow and turned to look at him. "We're two of a kind."

A thick, weighty silence settled between us as I left Wyatt to chew on my words and come to his own conclusions. Other than outright telling him I was interested in him, or grabbing him and kissing the ever-living shit out of his handsome face, I'd given him more than enough clues to put together that I was interested in him on another level, a physical level.

Once we hit Sheridan, it only took a few minutes to get to the small house off the main street that Miranda had converted into her rehab center. It was still early, so the typically sparse traffic was nonexistent. Driving through the deserted town made it feel like it was only the two of us in the entire world. That feeling was short-lived when a petite woman with curly white hair suddenly appeared on the porch of the building. Miranda waved at me, flashing a familiar, sad smile in my direction. Before my CO had taken his own life, she'd had wild red hair. It seemed like it went white overnight, taking a big chunk of her fiery personality with the color. She was a wonderful woman who'd lost more than she should have. She'd done more to help disabled and injured vets than any VA clinic I'd ever been to.

I hopped out of the SUV and went around to the passenger side to help Wyatt hop down. The other man gave me a look that might've killed a weaker man, but eventually he let me help him. He glared at me as I handed him his cane, his fair head jerking up when Miranda's soft chuckle drifted through the early morning air.

"What'd you bring me to play with, Sheriff?" She'd never lost her soft Texas drawl, a melodic tone I always found charming.

"Multiple gunshot wounds. Shattered ribs. An invasive infection that did some damage to his internal organs. Wrecked shoulder and blown-out knee. Pretty much every single part of him has some sort of battle scar except that pretty-boy face. You got your work cut out for you, Doc."

Wyatt couldn't hold back a gasp as I rattled off his laundry list of injuries. When I told him I was worried and curious about *everything* about him, he should have believed me. I spent more hours than I would ever admit prying information out of his little brother and Ten.

He introduced himself to Miranda in a quiet voice, looking slightly embarrassed.

Miranda clicked her tongue and reached out to shake Wyatt's hand. "I wish you had another reason to visit. You're right, ya know, he is too pretty to be dealing with all of that." She turned her attention back to me and gave me a hard look. "You owe me a dinner date. It's been too long, Rhodes."

I groaned when she used my real name, scowling at Wyatt when he burst out in a howl of laughter, "That's what Rodie is short for? I always wondered."

My mother gave me the name because she was young and thought it sounded dignified. I hated it. It was one more thing that made me stand out from everyone else when I was younger.

Before the conversation about my name could go any further, we were interrupted by another female voice. This one was sultry and seductive... or at least trying to be.

"Sheriff. I've been trying to track you down for days." I tried not to flinch when Delaney appeared out of nowhere. Her manicured fingers latched onto my arm and pulled me away from where I was hovering closer than appropriate to Wyatt.

"Let's grab breakfast and have a chat since you're in town so early."

I wanted to refuse and tell the persistent woman to take a hike. I saw the puzzled look cross Wyatt's face as he took in the overly familiar way she handled me and spoke to me, but I didn't get the chance.

Miranda squeezed Wyatt's hand and pulled him toward the steps of the building. She moved slowly and steadily to accommodate his uneven steps. "Let's get you checked out, Special Agent. You can fill me in on your past rehab, and we can go over any area you're particularly struggling with at the moment. I'll run you through some exercises and do some tests to see where you're at. Can't have one of Rhodes's brothers-in-arms fall apart on my watch." Miranda's kind eyes flicked over to me as I tried to subtly resist Delaney's pull on my arm. "Give me a couple hours with him, and bring breakfast for both of us when you come back." She flashed me a wink. "And I'm serious about that dinner date."

She helped Wyatt up the stairs, and my back teeth ground together watching them. I really wanted to be the one helping him.

The woman next to me scoffed and I felt her nails dig into my forearm. "What was that all about? You don't have something going on with that old woman, do you? Is she the reason you keep playing hard to get?"

It was all so ridiculous that all I could do was swear under my breath and tug my hat down lower on my forehead to hide my disappointed and annoyed expression.

"Fine, let's get this over with, Ms. Hall." The quicker I was done with her, the quicker I could get back to Wyatt.

CHAPTER 6

WYATT

"**Y**OU REALLY ARE QUITE the mess, aren't you, Special Agent Bryant?"

Miranda Connelly's voice was soothing and calm, as was her overall demeanor. She was cool and efficient, her questions direct and to the point. There was an innate sadness about her that made her seem older and more weathered than she actually looked. No matter how kind her smile was, it never reached her eyes. And regardless of how friendly and welcoming she sounded when she spoke, there was a hollow note in her tone, one I recognized from the worst part of my old job. I always hated having to notify a family that they'd lost someone. That empty echo in the physical therapist's voice came from having a huge chunk of your heart and happiness ripped away from you.

"Some of the damage is old. I worked undercover for a good portion of my career. Took a hit or two I should have taken better care of along the way." I forced a grin. "You know the military and the government train us to think we're invincible, so we play the part. It's expected."

The tiny woman scoffed and motioned for me to put my shirt back on. "You and Rhodes are cut from the exact same fabric. I told him there was no need for him to get into another career where he was bound to catch a bullet, but he didn't want to listen. Being in danger was more comfortable than having a sense of safety."

I cleared my throat as she bent her silvery head to scribble something in the chart she'd started for me. "Well, I'm sure you can tell I'm not in any position to get in the way of bad guys and bullets ever again. The DEA put me out to pasture, and I have no desire to go chasing after another badge." I was getting too old, and I was honestly too tired. I didn't know what was next for me, but I knew for sure that protecting and serving the public was no longer on the agenda.

She lifted her head and gave me another sorrowful smile. "I don't think you're as bad off as you think you are. If you commit to some pretty intense therapy and are open to alternative treatments, I think we can get that limp under control and most of your mobility and range of motion back. Fortunately, you are in excellent physical shape and aren't overly reliant on medications for pain management." She sighed and tapped the chart with the tip of her pen. "Often the hardest part for my clients is the detox from the endless drugs they've been given instead of focusing their recovery on actual care."

It was true. It was hardly a secret it was easier to medicate than to offer long-term treatment for serious injuries, be they physical or mental. With my mother's history of addiction and drug abuse, I very rarely let anything stronger than an over-the-counter painkiller into my system, and hated that I'd been forced to pop pain pill after pain pill the last couple of months.

The small woman turned to look at me with raised eyebrows. Her expression turned from thoughtful to curious as she gave me a suddenly unprofessional once over. "You really are very pretty. No wonder Rhodes called in a favor for you. I was surprised to hear from him last night. He always tries to check up on me at least once a week, but he's been so busy the last few months, I haven't seen very much of him."

Weirdly nervous at the inspection and weight of her words, I rubbed my hand across my jaw and looked down at the floor. "My younger brother has practically been adopted by the Warners. I'm sure Rodie called in the favor to keep the peace with them. I know things have been rocky between him and the family since he arrested Sutton last summer."

The older woman snorted and reached out to pat my good knee. "Honey, Rodie doesn't bend over backward for anyone. That boy is more stubborn than the oldest mule on any farm. His head is harder than titanium. If he felt like he was doing the right thing, there isn't a force on this Earth powerful enough to make him bend to someone else's will. He called in a favor because he was worried about you and he wanted to help."

I stiffened and felt the back of my neck heat up. The entire ride into town I'd been picking up different vibes from Rodie, and I couldn't get my mind off the way he'd blatantly checked me out when I opened the door. I've been around the block a time or two, so I knew what sexual interest from another man looked like. But I was confused as hell as to *why* Rodie Collins was looking at me that way.

Miranda patted my knee again and rolled away on her little chair. "Don't worry about the viper in the stilettos. She's been barking up the wrong tree for months. Eventually she's going to figure out she doesn't stand a chance in hell with our sheriff. That she-devil will never be his type."

That was a loaded sentence. There were a lot of reasons the pretty brunette might not be Rodie's type, and I didn't want to read too much into them. It felt safer to keep playing oblivious when it came to all the complexities surrounding Rodie. It was easier to treat him as a forbidden fantasy, rather than a reality I might be able to experience outside of my dirty imagination.

Maneuvering off the examination table, I reached for my cane and told the older woman, "I think you might have the wrong idea about me and Rodie. We're hardly even friends. I think he's just sympathetic to my situation because he's been there himself. I'm not concerned with whom he chooses to spend his time."

If I bothered being honest with myself, I had to admit I didn't like the way the brunette handled Rodie like he belonged to her. I didn't enjoy watching her run her painted fingernails up and down his arm, or the proprietary way she ordered him about as if she expected him to obey. I refused to acknowledge the feelings taking over my mind when I thought about the two of them together might hover pretty close to jealousy.

The therapist cocked her head and gave me a smile that finally lightened her eyes. "You're a stubborn one, as well, Special Agent Bryant. Like I said, cut from the same cloth." She chuckled under her breath and rolled herself over to her computer. "I'm going to put together a comprehensive rehab plan for you. I'll email it over in the next day or so. Even if you decide not to stay in Wyoming, I'm going to advise that you look at long-term care. If you don't want to do it with me, find someone you trust, and plan on having a regular routine. Your recovery will not be quick and easy, but there is definitely room for improvement."

I nodded. "I'll do that." I had no idea where I'd be once Webb and Ten finally decided to buy or build a house. I kept telling myself I was only here until my brother finally settled down. Only, Webb didn't seem to be in any hurry to make those big choices, and since I had nowhere else to be, all my future plans were up in the air. I liked Miranda, and I secretly liked that Rodie went out of his way to set up this appointment. It made me feel special and cared for, two things I hadn't felt from someone other than my brother in longer than I could remember.

Miranda was walking me out the front door, reminding me to do a series of stretches every day to help loosen the muscles in my lower back and strengthen my shoulder and leg, when Rodie appeared at the base of the stairs. His cowboy hat was tilted low on his forehead, so I couldn't see his face, but I could tell by the stiff set of his broad shoulders that his early morning meeting with the brunette woman had not gone well. Irritation rolled off the big man in waves.

He held up a brown paper bag in his hand and almost growled at Miranda, "Breakfast."

She clicked her tongue and waved me toward Rodie. "Feed him. I'm fine. I have another client in a few minutes. It was good to see you this morning, Rhodes. Don't you dare forget our dinner date."

Rodie's wide shoulders slumped slightly and he nodded. "Yes, ma'am. I'll call you when I get a free hour or two. Thanks for getting my boy in so quickly."

I froze mid-step, head snapping up and eyes locking on Rodie's. He did not just call me his "boy" … did he?

I stuck a finger in my ear and wiggled it around to make sure I wasn't hearing things. Balanced with my cane and one foot, I nearly toppled down the last few steps. Rodie caught me effortlessly, something I realized he'd done with increasing frequency since my arrival in Wyoming. I muttered an embarrassed thanks and went to move away, but was brought up short when he set a warm, steady hand low on my back.

"I hope you like breakfast burritos." He started to guide me toward his marked SUV. "I tried to grab something that would be fairly easy in the car."

Man, he was considerate. Far more so than I'd been toward him. "Anything is fine. You didn't have to get me anything."

He grunted as he pulled open the door for me. "I dragged you away from the ranch before Brynn could feed you. I can't bring you back with an empty stomach; she'd have my head on a platter."

Once I was settled in the passenger seat with the bag of food on my lap, Rodie made his way around to the other side of the vehicle and climbed in. He tugged off his hat and tossed it in the back seat before starting the car. As if my hand suddenly had a mind of its own, my fingers involuntarily reached out to lift the reddish-brown strands that had flattened to his head under the weight of the hat.

His hair was super soft and looked even redder when it wasn't smashed against his skull. We both made a shocked sound when we realized what I was doing and I jerked my fingers away like his head was on fire. Blushing furiously, I quickly looked away and stammered out an apology.

"Um, oh fuck, sorry about that." I didn't have an excuse for the action, so I simply refused to meet his eyes and hoped I hadn't crossed a line or made him uncomfortable.

Rodie sighed heavily and, out of the corner of my eye, I watched him ruffle the rest of his hair. Now that I knew how nice it felt to the touch, my fingers tingled and I had to fight the urge to reach out and replace his hands with my own. Damn, I'd definitely made things uncomfortable.

Rodie started the SUV and asked, "How did things go with Miranda?"

I fidgeted with the bag of food on my lap and answered truthfully, "Yeah, uh, she's great. She was honest about what could and couldn't be improved. There's a loss of musculature no one can do anything about, but she thinks she can get my limp under control and full range of motion back in my shoulder if I commit to treatment." I shrugged slightly. "I don't know how long I'm going to be in Sheridan, but while I am here, I think I'll make the effort to go see her."

"That's good news."

I thought Rodie was going to be more excited about the positive prognosis, but he seemed distracted, his tone was almost flat.

Setting the food on the floor between my feet, I twisted in the seat as much as I could and faced him.

"Rodie, are you okay? Did something happen during your breakfast meeting with that woman?" I didn't realize it until right then, but I'd gotten used to the intensity of his attention when we were together. Usually, I felt like I was the only thing he could see, and that all of his focus was on me when it was just the two of us. I hated that it totally rubbed me the wrong way that he wouldn't even look at me right now, even though I was speaking directly to him.

It took a moment for him to reply. When he did, his voice was low and raspier than normal.

"Delaney informed me the mayor is actively looking for someone to run against me." He snorted and rapped his hand on the steering wheel. A sour expression crossed his face as he muttered, "She offered to run interference for me, but only if I agree to sleep with her. It was an uncomfortable, unpleasant conversation all around. I'm not happy I'm suddenly in the middle of the mayor's games. I don't like having my job being dangled in front of me like a carrot." He turned his head to look at me. "But I am glad you got good news from Miranda. I knew if anyone could patch you up, it would be her."

I went still, and my next words sprang out of my mouth before my common sense could catch up.

"If the job means that much to you, why don't you just sleep with her? She was attractive enough, if you like that type." It was a knee-jerk reaction, a defensive maneuver to keep Rodie firmly in the do-not-touch category. I should've known better. This was not a man you challenged lightly.

The SUV jerked to the side of the road. No big deal since the traffic was minimal and we were far enough out of the city limits as we headed toward the Warner ranch. Dust flew up and surrounded the windows as the man next to me went stone still for a second before suddenly exploding into motion.

He clicked open my seat belt as he leaned closer to me, almost crowding me into the door.

One of Rodie's hands locked on the front of my shirt and the other landed on the side of my neck. I prayed he couldn't feel the way my pulse kicked to life under his palm. However, I knew there was no hiding the way my breath caught or the way I shivered.

"Why don't I sleep with her?" Rodie sounded furious, his voice nothing more than a low rumble. "Did you really just ask me that, Wyatt?"

I lifted a hand and wrapped my fingers around his wrist. I felt my eyes go wide when I realized his pulse was hammering just as furiously as mine.

Glaring, green eyes sliced into me as his head moved closer to mine. My lips parted without permission and I watched in frozen fascination as Rodie's nostrils flared in response.

"You know why I *won't* sleep with her. You know exactly why I *can't* sleep with her, even if it means losing my position as sheriff. Stop playing dumb. It doesn't suit you at all." The warning was clear, and so was his intent.

I blinked and squeezed his wrist, not sure if I wanted to pull him off me, or tug him closer. "I won't ever make assumptions about something like that. I won't think anything without empirical proof." Partly because I was an investigator by trade, but more because I'd learned to be careful from experience. When I was younger, I'd been burned more than once by thinking someone was interested in me just because I really wanted them to be. Some boys liked to play games, and I was not about to be a pawn. Not after my mother played me over and over again.

"Empirical proof?" Rodie barked the words, eyes narrowing on mine. "Fine. Here is your empirical proof, Special Agent."

I knew he was going to kiss me.

I sensed it all the way down to my bones.

I could have evaded, or pushed him away, but I didn't.

I wasn't sure I liked this man, and was pretty sure I didn't entirely trust him. However, when his lips landed on mine, there was no denying I liked the way he kissed and I wanted more of it. More of him, because it suddenly seemed like an option for me to have him.

CHAPTER 7

RODIE

TASTED HUNGER AND SURRENDER on Wyatt's lips as I leaned into him, forgetting where I was and *who* I was the instant my mouth touched his.

I didn't expect him to practically melt under my hands. I was anticipating more of a fight and a truckload of reluctance. What I got was warm, wet, pliable lips pressed hungrily against mine, shaking fingers holding onto whatever part of me he could reach, and a shy flick of his tongue when I leaned closer and pulled him farther over the middle console of the SUV.

One of us gasped, but I wasn't sure who because I couldn't think, or feel, or see anything beyond the places where we touched. I'd been alone for such a long time and purposely distanced myself from others. There was something about Wyatt Bryant that pulled at me from the very beginning. Instead of pushing him away, I found myself wanting to get as close to him as possible. I lived my entire life being someone else for others. This kiss, this brief, stolen, heated moment on the side of a dusty road outside of Sheridan, Wyoming was the only time I'd taken something simply for myself. I kissed Wyatt because I *had* to kiss him. I felt like I would die if I didn't get a chance to taste him, to feel him pressed up against me, at least once. The need to shake his unwavering control and rigid restraint had been hounding me and keeping me awake at night since we'd met.

I placed one of my hands on the side of his neck, using my thumb to tilt back his sharp chin so I could go at his delectable mouth from another angle. I felt his pulse pound under the weight of my palm, and his fingers tightened almost painfully around my wrist. I was waiting for a protest or for him to jerk away. I was properly stunned when Wyatt deepened the kiss, the tip of his tongue skating expectantly along the seam of my lips. I opened up obediently and tasted coffee and something minty as his skilled tongue twirled against mine.

The fingers of his free hand suddenly threaded through the longer strands of hair at the nape of my neck. It wasn't a gentle caress or a tender stroke. He tugged on a handful of hair, returning my forceful handling. He was as actively involved in the moment as I was. He was kissing me back voraciously, taking as much as he was giving, forgetting for a stolen moment the pain and sadness that had brought him here. Never in any of my lurid fantasies, did Wyatt come across as a passionate, hungry lover. I always imagined him being cool and composed, even in the bedroom.

I was wrong.

He was hot... everywhere.

His hands, where they held me, felt like they were made of flames.

His mouth, doing its best to devour mine, was warm and insistent.

His uneven, jagged breaths were steamy and sweet.

There wasn't anything cool about him, and all that heat was scrambling my normal sense of self-preservation. Whom I was attracted to and with whom I went to bed was something I kept firmly off the table for discussion. Yet, here I was out in the open, in my marked sheriff's vehicle, losing myself to the most physically and emotionally intense make out session I'd ever experienced.

Kissing Wyatt was like having my first kiss with a boy all over again. There was something new and fresh about it. Something eye-opening and life-changing. It was the kind of kiss that showed what had been missing from my life. The kind of kiss that could change me.

Wyatt's fingers continued to tug at my hair, and his teeth dragged along the soft inside of my lower lip. The interior of the vehicle was filled with the sounds of heavy breathing and intermittent gulps and gasps of pleasure. We were lost in our own little world where our secrets and differences didn't matter. It was a place I could've happily stayed forever.

One of Wyatt's hands dropped to my thigh. The muscle automatically tightened, and every part of my body was vibrating in anticipation. The twisted position in my seat was already uncomfortable, but the way his touch made my body harden and throb behind my zipper pushed things closer to unbearable.

I slid my palm down the length of his neck, letting my fingers dip into the collar of his plain black t-shirt. The tender exploration stilled when the tips of my fingers skated over the rough, lifted skin of one of his many surgical scars. It was a stark reminder of how close he'd come to no longer being here. A reminder of what I might've missed out on if I kept dancing around the fact that I wanted him, even though we saw things very differently. I desperately wanted to believe our similarities would do more to bring us together than our differences would do to pull us apart.

I dragged my hand down his strong chest until I had his rapid, strong heartbeat under the palm of my hand. I loved the way his lips felt underneath mine. I was quickly getting addicted to the soft, sexy sounds he made each time the slant and direction of the kiss changed. I liked the subtle strength coming from his battered body. And I liked the rhythmic, steady beat of his heart the most because it meant he survived. That we'd both survived. Because, despite the odds and my own reservations, I was here to feel his quickened pulse. He was still here with me; we had time to figure this thing out between us. No matter how difficult and challenging it might be.

Wyatt's hand started to slide slowly up my thigh. My body reacted quickly, almost embarrassingly so. I wanted nothing more than to feel his fingertips touch the hard, taut flesh pressing insistently against the zipper of my jeans.

Only, it wasn't the right time, and definitely not the right place. The radio in my car squawked to life as the dispatcher called for a deputy to check on a possible robbery at one of the family-owned pharmacies in town. The sound made us jump away from one another as reality crashed down around us.

I absolutely shouldn't be kissing anyone while I was on duty. And I definitely shouldn't be kissing another man out in the open where anyone could pass by and see. Especially not with the mayor breathing down my neck and the election right around the corner.

Wyatt pulled his hands away like he'd been caught touching a priceless piece of art at a museum. He shoved one of his hands through his golden hair and blinked his pretty blue eyes at me before barking, "What in the holy hell was that?"

I dragged my hands down my face and reached out to start the SUV back up. I also radioed that I heard the call about the robbery but was on my way out of town and wouldn't be back for an hour. The dispatcher copied as I pulled the vehicle back onto the road and headed toward the Warner ranch.

Wyatt made a strangled sound and lifted his fingers to his kiss-swollen lips. "Seriously, Rodie, what was that? You being attracted to men is one thing, you being attracted to *me* is an entirely different thing. No fucking way are you going to convince me that, even if you are gay, I'm your type." He snorted and shook his head. "Plus, I don't play around with people who hang out in the closet. It's way too dark and crowded in there, and I worked way too hard to fight my way out despite my mother, the military, and the DEA."

I could hear the judgment and censure in his tone. It set my teeth on edge and chased away some of the soft, warm feelings still swirling around in my blood from that kiss.

"I'm not in or out of any closet. I keep my private life exactly that, private. It's no one's business whom I go to bed with." That was how I'd always lived my life and I didn't think I'd be changing that mentality anytime soon.

When I was younger, no one cared enough to ask what I was up to. My mother barely acknowledged my existence, and it was easier for everyone involved if I made as little fuss as possible while under my aunt and uncle's roof. I was a shadow, being as unobtrusive and as quiet as possible. When I got older, the need for self-preservation kicked in. Unlike Cam, I did my best to blend in. Even when I knew for certain the cute cowgirls and female cheerleaders weren't ever going to do anything for me, I kept the knowledge to myself. Then, much like Wyatt had mentioned, I knew my career path in the military would go much more smoothly if I kept my personal preferences to myself. Advancements in inclusivity had been made over the years, but the military was never going to be as progressive as it claimed to be, so who I spent time with and who I shared my body with were things I kept on lockdown. I never felt like I lived a life in the closet, but I could freely admit I was less than honest when it came to where my heart wandered.

Wyatt scoffed and I watched as he rubbed his palms up and down his thighs. He was upset, but it was nice to know he'd been as affected by the kiss as I was.

"You're right. It isn't anyone's business, but we've known each other for a while now, and you've been aware of who I am from the first moment we met. You keep mentioning how much we have in common, so you could have mentioned exactly *how* similar we are. You could've mentioned you were interested in me at some point along the way." The words sounded sullen, and sure enough, he had an adorable pout on his face. With his full lips and sharp jawline, it was no surprise that he was even pretty when he pouted.

"I didn't come right out and tell you I was interested, but I've been showing you. You just weren't paying attention, Wyatt." It was true. I'd been dropping hints that I would very much like to get naked with him since Cy and Leo's wedding. But life kept interfering and pulling him away. I never got a chance to make a play, and now here he was, hurt and healing. The timing was never in my favor... until now.

Almost as if he didn't hear me, he blurted out, "And what about Cam? Do you know what that kid's been through, how horrible he's been treated just because he's gay? Nothing you and I have been through can compare to the horrors that boy has seen. Do you know how good it would be for him to have another role model, another grown, successful gay man in his life? You could make a huge difference in his life if you were more honest about your own."

I sighed and cranked my head to look at him as the entrance to the ranch got closer. "We all have different experiences and reasons for living the way we do. I don't think it's fair for you to judge me. There isn't one right way to be a happy, healthy gay man, Wyatt. You should know that." I didn't like that he was unerringly poking at some of my most tender places. Could I do more? Should I do more? What would I lose if I did? Those questions had haunted me for a long time. Fear of change and of the unknown was a real bitch.

He made a noise again and narrowed his eyes at me. "Okay, but are you happy and healthy, Rodie?"

Was I? Depended on the day. But I could honestly say I'd felt happier and healthier when I'd had his mouth pressed against mine a few moments ago.

I narrowed my eyes back at him and growled, "What about you? When was the last time you were actually happy, Special Agent?"

Wyatt stiffened and I could feel waves of tension coming off of him. A heavy, thick silence descended on us, and it wasn't until the massive ranch house and big barn on the Warner's property came into view several moments later that Wyatt spoke.

"The last time I was happy was when I came out of surgery and Webb told me our mother was dead." He sucked in a breath and then let out a dry, brittle laugh. The sound actually hurt to hear. "Instead of being relieved I was alive, I was excited she was gone and could no longer play her games with me and Webb. She was a terrible mother, and an awful person, but what does it say about me that I was glad she was no longer a threat? Doesn't that make me even worse than she was?"

I pulled to a stop in front of his bunkhouse, turning so we were facing each other. Clearly, we both had ghosts from the past haunting us, some hanging on for dear life. He might seem like he had his shit together, but at the moment, he was just as messed up on the inside as he was on the outside. Wyatt reached for the door handle, his voice quiet and serious when he told me, "I liked kissing you, Sheriff, but I'm not sure I actually like *who* you are. I'm not entirely sure what to do with that."

I heaved a deep sigh and dropped my forehead to the steering wheel. My radio crackled to life once again, and I knew I had to get back to work and stop chasing after my almost-impossible fantasy.

"We all learn how to survive in whatever way works best for us. You did it by putting your mother firmly in the 'enemy' category and distancing yourself from the damage she could do. I did it by becoming whoever I needed to be in order to succeed. Maybe we both need to figure out who we really are without the expectations of anyone else hanging over our heads." I turned my head to look at him and was surprised to find him watching me with intent, quizzical eyes.

"What if who you really are is a man who wants to be open about who he is and who he loves? How are you going to handle that? How is this town going to adjust?" He shook his head again and shoved open the door. "Thanks for the ride and for introducing me to Miranda. I think this is as far as we can go together. This is who I really am, Rodie. There is no better version of me hidden somewhere."

My hand reached out to grab the hem of his t-shirt before I could think better of it. Wyatt paused, half in, half out of the SUV. His eyebrows lifted and his lips twisted into a pensive frown. My eyebrows shot up and I gave him a lopsided grin.

"I'm not complaining about this version of you. This is the version I wanted to kiss. This is the version I jerk off to every other night. This is the version I want to take to bed and keep there until neither one of us can walk straight. There is nothing wrong with who you are, Wyatt. There's nothing wrong with who I am either. I just think it's possible that the right person in your life might make you want to change in unexpected ways."

He made a confused face as he pulled away and climbed the rest of the way out of the SUV.

"You think you're the right person for me, Sheriff?"

He made it sound like it was impossible, so I flashed him a grin and told him with a fair amount of certainty, "No, I'm not saying that. What I'm saying is, I'm pretty sure you're the right person for me, Special Agent."

CHAPTER 8

WYATT

"SO, WHAT DO YOU think?"

Webb's voice was more excited than I'd ever heard it. He sounded like what I assume a normal kid sounded like on Christmas morning. We'd never had the luxury of presents under a tree. Hell, we were lucky if there was bread and peanut butter in the pantry on any given holiday. When we were younger, our mom's family, our aunts and uncles, did their best to include Webb and me in celebrations, but my mother, being the sick and twisted woman she was, insisted we didn't need frivolous things like toys and games. She haughtily told the rest of the family her kids weren't going to be spoiled brats, and we weren't. No, we were deeply scared and emotionally scarred. We grew up doing whatever we had to in order to survive and fighting every single day so we could stay together.

I looked around the crumbling farmhouse Webb was practically giddy over. When he told me he finally found a place he and Ten agreed on, I expected more than a house that looked like it was barely standing. The whole place needed to be bulldozed and rebuilt, but Webb was looking at the rotting walls and collapsing beams as if the house were a true gem.

I kicked at a loose floorboard with the toe of my sneaker and winced when the entire plank lifted, nails sticking out in all directions.

"Needs some work, kiddo." I didn't have the heart to tell him the whole place screamed 'money pit.' "I can't believe Ten approves of a house that needs so much renovation." She wasn't a patient woman by any means, and she was super busy. She was always on call, so there was no way she could help Webb breathe life back into this building. Not that my little brother was Mr. Fix-It. He was handy enough with the basics, but this decrepit relic needed an entire overhaul.

Webb chuckled and walked over to a broken window so he could drag a finger through the dust accumulated on the grimy pane. "She's actually found this piece of property. She's more interested in the land than the house. I guess it's been on the market for a while, but the price was outrageous. The owner recently passed away and the family wants to ditch the property as quickly as possible." He shrugged. "I have more money than I know what to do with. Might as well invest it in the future. There's enough land here to build a house, a barn, and another house." He turned and lifted his eyebrows at me. "There's enough land to put down roots and create something that's ours. Something no one can come and take away from us. Isn't that what you've always dreamed of?"

I tapped the end of my cane on the uneven floor and refused to meet Webb's excited gaze.

"You think I'm going to stay in Wyoming?" I kept my voice even, but I couldn't stop my fingers from tightening on the handle of the cane. "Did I give you the impression that I was here to stay, Webb?" I didn't know what I was doing with my life, but I sure as shit was not going to be a burden to my little brother when he'd just gotten himself straightened out.

Webb turned to face me, a frown digging deep lines into his handsome face. "I honestly don't know what you're doing anymore, Wyatt. You seem like you're drifting from one day to the next. I can't remember the last time I heard you laugh or saw you genuinely smile. I feel like you're looking through me half the time when I talk to you. Would it be the worst thing in the world to settle down here? Would it be so bad to have me and Ten as neighbors? Is it so hard to imagine having family close by? Are you scared of relying on me, of letting me help you? Am I really that unreliable in your eyes?"

I took a second to process what he was saying. I didn't realize I'd been refusing his help and that my ingrained independence was hurting him.

"Webb," I started to apologize, but he held up a hand to stop me.

"Don't. I know you aren't trying to be an asshole. I know you're just trying to figure out what your life looks like now that you aren't chasing down drug smugglers. I understand that a simple life in the middle of nowhere might not be what you want, but *I'm* here." He looked me directly in the eyes, frown deepening. "I don't get why it hasn't even crossed your mind to stay where I am. We've both been on the move for so long, running from so much, now we have a chance to stop and be in the same place at the same time and just be," He shook his head and I felt my heart seize in my chest. "I hate that it feels like you're trying to get away from me."

"No." The denial was automatic and full of force. Webb was my favorite person on the planet. I'd given up my entire childhood to make sure he was standing in front of me now in one piece and a mostly respectable man. I leaned heavily on the cane and looked down at the mangled board I'd kicked. "I love you, Webb. I only want the best for you."

And the best wasn't him rearranging his life to take care of me because mine was in shambles. I knew how hard and draining it could be to suddenly be responsible for the well-being of someone else, even someone you loved with your whole heart.

Webb started to pace back and forth, cowboy boots clicking furiously on the brittle wooden floors. "And I want the best for you, Wyatt. Do you think I was blind to the sacrifices you made for me when we were younger? Do you really believe I don't know the lengths you went to protect me from Mom and the rest of the world when I was too young and immature to protect myself? I don't know how you could ever think I'd view you as a burden. You never treated me that way, even when I was an annoying teenager getting into trouble on purpose. You're my brother. You're my only family. I owe you everything, and you won't let me give you anything in return. If you were in my shoes, wouldn't you want to give something back to the person who made you into the man you are today? No matter how big or how small?"

I dragged a hand down my face, suddenly feeling exhausted. "I didn't realize how important all of this was to you. I honestly thought you just wanted to keep an eye on me until I was back on my feet, that we'd both go back to living our own lives. I never even considered that you'd want me to hang around."

Webb scoffed and whipped his Stetson off his head. I was still getting used to the cowboy version of my brother, but I had to admit the boots, belt buckles, and tight jeans suited him. So did the hard, honest work and the love of a good woman. Somehow, Webb had landed in the middle of the life I'd always dreamed of having. There was a part of me that could admit I was jealous, but there was a bigger, louder part screaming at me not to screw up all the good things Webb had going for him now.

It was just how things happened when you were a Bryant.

Things would seem like they were leveling out, gaining some sense of normalcy, and then *boom*, it all went to hell. Quickly. I'd learned at an early age not to rest on my laurels and never to let my guard down. Even when it came to my younger brother.

"I started thinking about the future as soon as you went missing." Webb waved a hand around the house, his frustration palpable. "You were the reason I ended up here. If that case hadn't gone south, if you hadn't gone missing on the Warner's property," he shivered dramatically. "I never would have met Ten. I wouldn't have found a career I enjoy. I would never have found a place where I finally felt like I belong. It was like we were meant to come to this exact spot."

I tossed my head back and groaned at the collapsing ceiling. "I get that you feel like this is where you were meant to be, that fate played a big hand in bringing you here, but we're different, Webb." I gave him a pointed look. "You took to the culture and the lifestyle here like a duck to water. You realize it wouldn't be the same for me, right?" He didn't need me to remind him how much Cam stuck out in this small town, and it wasn't my place to tell him Rodie was practically living a double life. "I may like to handle things on my own, but that doesn't mean I want to be *alone*." I might be letting go of my dream of a traditional marriage and family, but there was no way in hell that I planned on giving up sex. Especially after that kiss with the sheriff. The man had a talented, tricky tongue, and rough, powerful hands. I wanted to feel them both again, without the barrier of clothes and the police radio interruption. That didn't seem likely, though, with the way we ended things. My self-preservation instincts were too strong, and just like always, I pushed whomever was trying to get close away before they had the chance to hurt me. To disappoint me. To abandon me.

I'd woken up more than once with my hand wrapped around my very hard cock and Rodie's name on my lips. I could almost picture the arrogant gleam in those green eyes if he had any clue what I was getting up to with him in mind.

Webb sighed heavily and pointed a finger at me. "You don't have to fit in. The people who matter most know who you are and love you no matter what. And the only reason you would be lonely is because you aren't letting anyone get close enough to keep you company. Who knows who you might meet around here? Plus, the internet exists, Wyatt. You can find a date in two seconds if you really want to. Stop making excuses." He dropped his hand and walked over to me. He reached out and put a hand on my good shoulder. He squeezed lightly and gave me a crooked grin. "We have a lot of bad memories between us, big brother. I get it if you need to get away from me in order to leave those behind. I guess I always hoped the good memories we made were big enough to blur out the rest."

Man, the kid was good at going right for the heart. No wonder he made such a good con-man when he was living on the wrong side of the law. Rarely did he turn that slick manipulation and those puppy dog eyes on me, but it was effective when he did.

I swore under my breath and shot a hand out to clasp the back of his neck. We were the same height, so it was easy enough to tug him forward until our foreheads touched.

"You really want to take on this monster?" The idea of my baby brother building a house from the ground up was so strange and scary, I still couldn't get my head around it.

"I want to stay here. I want a place that feels like home. I want Ten to know every single piece of wood in the place we live together has a piece of us on it. I'm going to do this, with or without your support." All the previous excitement had bled from his voice and I felt like a total asshole. We'd never had much, and now that Webb had something he clearly wanted and was willing to fight for, I was the jerk trying to point out everything wrong with his dreams. I was so used to rescuing him from himself, I didn't know what to do with the version of

Webb who could not only save himself but save me along the way.

I knocked our foreheads together, causing Webb to give me a playful scowl. "Buy the property. Build the dream house. I'll stick around at least until the foundation is poured. Give me some time to get my feet underneath me. I promise that once I do, I won't use them to run away. If you are bound and determined to give me a place on your property, know that even if I don't stay forever, I will always come back to you. Getting you to this point is the best thing I've ever done. I'm prouder of you than I am of anything else in my life, baby brother."

We both got a little choked up and stayed silent for a long moment. Webb was the first to pull away, giving me a light shove, then immediately reaching out to help me keep my balance when I teetered for a second.

"Thank you for pretending to let me take care of you, even if you don't need me to, Wyatt."

He'd done a much better job at moving on from everything that still held me down. I liked to pretend I'd grown and lived a life beyond all the horrible things my mother had planted in my head and tried to make me believe about myself, but this conversation with Webb was a clear reminder I still tended to see myself through my mother's eyes. She was the last person I should be allowing to judge me, but old habits died hard.

I nodded and started to follow him carefully around the house as he pointed out some of the vintage fixtures he planned on keeping and reusing.

I poked him in the butt with the end of my cane and muttered, "I can't believe you're encouraging me to internet date. Do you know what kind of weirdos are on those sites?" And how many of the men on them were only looking for a quick hookup. When I was younger, that was all well and good, but as I got older and more disenchanted, I wanted more.

Webb chuckled and looked at me over his shoulder with a raised brow. "I don't think you have to look too far for someone to spend time with, big bro. You and the sheriff seem like you're getting along pretty well."

I balked in surprise. "What?"

Webb laughed in my face. "Come on. You think I can't tell there's something going on there? Rodie keeps to himself and he's hard to read, except when it comes to you. He's been watching you like a hawk since the two of you first met."

"No, you're wrong." He had to be. I would've noticed if Rodie had been interested before... wouldn't I? Plus, all we did was disagree and butt heads. Maybe my little brother was mistaking animosity for sexual tension... though that kiss had been anything but disagreeable.

"I'm not wrong. I know people. That's what kept me alive when I lived on the streets. And I pay especially close attention to anyone paying attention to you."

He really could read almost anyone who crossed his path. He used the skill to rip off the unsuspecting back in the day and keep himself safe when his life was filled with predators. The average Joe might not suspect Rodie played for the same team I did, but there was a solid chance my baby brother had picked up on subtle clues anyone else would miss.

"Rodie was paying attention to me?" I didn't really understand why that knowledge sent a little thrill shooting through my blood.

Webb made a disgusted noise and rolled his eyes at me. "He purposely riles you up and pushes your buttons. He wants a reaction out of you, good or bad. He was obviously worried when you were shot, and he keeps finding reasons to be where you are. I don't know much about the man, but I do know he doesn't look at you the way he looks at everyone else."

How did he look at me? And how did I miss it? If it was the same way he looked at me when he walked in on me when I was half-naked, then I'd obviously been missing out. Rodie was hot, but when he looked like he wanted to eat me alive, his gaze was on another level.

However, none of that changed the fact we lived our lives very differently, and as similar as we were, those differences honestly seemed insurmountable. I could barely walk without falling over. No way was I up to breaking down the walls of insecurity Rodie hid behind. I was too tired and injured to offer him a hand up and over my own walls.

So, even if he looked at me like I was special and touched me like he never wanted to let me go, it wasn't enough for me to risk letting him get close enough to hurt me.

I was better off alone. I was safer that way.

CHAPTER 9

RODIE

IT HAD ALREADY BEEN a long, stressful day. I'd been called out to two different domestic disturbance calls, a missing persons call, and I'd had to break up a happy hour fistfight at one of the bars on Main Street. I was also missing two deputies because of a stomach bug going around, and I could tell colder weather was on the way because my knee ached. Every time I moved, my joints popped in a painful symphony. Needless to say, I was ready to file my reports and head home. I was exhausted and knew tomorrow wasn't going to be any easier, especially if the illness hitting town spread to more of my staff.

I was stopped by one of the night patrol guys as soon as I entered the sheriff's office. He had a concerned look on his face, which only deepened when he took in my weary, aggravated appearance.

"I tried to tell them to come back tomorrow, but they wouldn't listen." The young deputy fiddled with the badge on his shirt as he looked down at the toes of his polished boots. "I wasn't sure how to throw the mayor out."

I tossed my head back and groaned loudly toward the ceiling. Dealing with the uppity mayor was the last thing I wanted to do right now. Lowering my head, I rubbed my tired eyes and asked, "You said 'they' wouldn't listen. Who else is in there with him?" I had a good guess, but wanted to prepare myself, because Delaney Hall had been trying my patience in an unreal way as of late. Her actions were starting to border on harassment, and it was getting much more difficult to play nice for the sake of my job.

"The mayor and his assistant. I told them you wouldn't be back until later, but they insisted on waiting. They've been back in your office for about an hour."

I swore and rubbed at my temple where I could feel the start of a headache building. Of course, the mayor would make himself at home in my office. Luckily, I managed to clean the place up after Delaney's last ambush, so there was nothing laying around that shouldn't be seen by non-law enforcement eyes.

I gave the young deputy a fist bump and told him to be careful on his patrol tonight. It wasn't a full moon, but it sure felt like it. I took off my hat before stepping into the office. Shoving my fingers through my hair as I glared at my unwelcome guests, I demanded, "Why are you here so late?" I'd lost my patience with propriety and respect after the abysmal way this man had handled the knowledge that his son was a bigot and a bully. It disgusted me that the bad apple didn't fall far from the tree.

My back teeth ground together, and I could feel a muscle twitch in my cheek as I took in how the mayor made himself comfortable behind my desk. He was leaning back in my chair, the heels of his expensive cowboy boots propped up on the edge. Delaney had a hip propped up on the corner, head bent, attention directed at her phone as I stalked into the space which normally felt like home.

"You're a busy fella, aren't you, Sheriff?" The mayor shifted his considerable bulk, feet hitting the floor with a thud. "I guess crime waits for no man."

He flashed me a grin that made my skin crawl. I tossed my Stetson to the center of the desk and crossed my arms over my chest.

"You could've made an appointment instead of waiting for me to get back. My job is to protect and serve the people of Sheridan, that means I need to be where they are. It's good for them to see the sheriff enforcing the law and a good reminder to those who don't uphold it that they're never far away from getting caught. I don't spend much time behind that desk." In fact, I hated sitting around and filling out paperwork. I'd much rather be on patrol and spot check that my guys were diligently doing their duty, rather than be nothing more than a figurehead. I was always a hands-on kind of guy, even before becoming the sheriff of this town.

"People make appointments to see me, not the other way around." The mayor climbed to his feet and shoved his hands deep into the pockets of his dress pants. He gave me a cool look that quickly turned into a smirk as he informed me, "We just wanted to stop by and let you know, personally, that we've found the perfect candidate to run against you for sheriff."

This ridiculous show all made sense now. Normally this man wouldn't wait around for anyone. He was too self-important and arrogant to hang out in my less-than-spotless office without a specific reason. He wanted to make sure I heard the news from him and no one else. The man was waiting for some kind of reaction, or for me to drop to my knees and plead with him to take me back under his wing.

Yeah, hell would freeze over first.

I wasn't going to give him the satisfaction of responding in an outrageous way. Instead, I dipped my chin in acknowledgment and told him, "Congratulations. The election is right around the corner. Good luck getting this town to rally around someone new and unknown." I'd had to do that exact thing when I first ran for the job, so I knew exactly how hard it was to get the locals on board with change.

Delaney finally looked up from her phone. Her smile was particularly smug and just a little bit vicious.

"Ahh, but we didn't find someone new and unknown. No, the man running against you was born and raised right here in Sheridan. He's got roots buried deep in this town's soil, and a name that will carry a lot of weight with voters." She tossed her long, dark hair over her shoulder and tapped her painted nails on the top of my desk. "He's also got a squeaky-clean record, and no questionable actions against him."

Refusing to ask for a name, or play their tired game, I lowered one of my arms and motioned toward the door. "Sounds like you found yourself a ringer. Good job. If that's all you dropped by to tell me…" I waved my hand toward the door again. "I have reports to fill out, and I haven't had dinner yet." I was just short of being outright rude, but the hold on my temper and my patience was loosening rapidly.

"Byron is going to run against you." Delaney provided the name of her ex-husband with a bit of glee as the mayor chuckled. "He's got a lot of friends in the right places. He'll make a great sheriff."

And he would literally do whatever she told him to do. It was no secret the man was still head over heels in love with his ex-wife. He'd been against the divorce and fought valiantly to not only save his marriage, but to win his wife back once the papers were signed. He wasn't a bad guy, but he was dumb as a box of rocks, and if he ended up winning the election, there was no way he would be anything more than a name embossed on the door. The mayor and Delaney would call all the shots in Sheridan, which didn't bode well for anyone who was slightly different, like Cam.

"I've met Byron a time or two. He seems like a stand-up guy, but does he have any experience in law enforcement?" I would eat my hat if the man knew even the basics of the penal code.

The mayor snorted and rocked back on his heels. "He's got a master's degree, and he did a stint in the Reserves when he was younger. He might not have the background you do, but he's good with people, and he's not scared to do the right thing. He's vested in keeping Sheridan the way it always has been. He understands there are some forms of *change* we're just not interested in embracing."

I bit back a frustrated sigh. That was exactly what I was afraid of.

The mayor continued to smirk. "I believe Byron would've handled the situation at the high school much better. And he has nothing to hide. Can you say the same, Sheriff Collins? If we go digging in your closet, are we going to find more than skeletons? You seemed awfully invested in taking that gay kid's side."

A chill raced up my spine, but I wasn't going to give this man the satisfaction of knowing he was poking around a little too close to my most tender spots.

"Maybe you should just abdicate the position before things get really ugly for you, Rodie." The threat was clear. He wanted to take me down and have the sheriff's department in the palm of his hand, and he wasn't going to play fair in order to reach his goal.

My stomach churned, and I instantly regretted ever taking his support and endorsement.

"Do what you gotta do. I'm gonna let the job I've done and my service record speak for themselves. I choose to have faith that the majority of people don't think in the same backwards, antiquated way as you and your family." I moved toward the door. Pulling it open, I inclined my head to the interior of the station. "Now, if you'll both excuse me, I have some work to finish up."

The mayor sauntered out of the office as if he'd won some kind of victory. Delaney was much slower to leave. She paused in the door, dragging one of her fingers across my chest and stopping to tap on my badge. I shifted away from her and narrowed my eyes.

"Stop touching me without my permission, Ms. Hall. I don't like it, and it's very unprofessional." I was starting to get very sympathetic to any woman who'd ever had to face this kind of sexual harassment in the workplace. Not that I hadn't been sympathetic before, but now I had first-hand knowledge of how embarrassing and frustrating unwanted attention from someone who could directly impact your career was. I made a mental note to make sure my department was up to date on all their necessary sexual harassment training. I never wanted anyone under my command to feel the way I was feeling right now.

"This attitude of yours is the problem, Rodie." She lifted her eyebrows at me, but moved away when I purposely pushed her hand away from me. "I can get Byron to drop out of the election. He's wrapped around my little finger and only agreed to run against you after I asked him to. Give me what I want, and all this can go away." She winked at me as I shuddered in revulsion.

"I've tried to be reasonable and polite, but you keep pushing. I'm not interested in you, Delaney, not now, not ever. You aren't my type, and even if it means I lose the job that means everything to me, I still won't sleep with you." I shook my head at her, reaching for the door so I could close it on her disgruntled face. "Stop selling yourself short. You know you're attractive. You know there are several other men in this town who would gladly give anything to have a shot with you. The only reason you won't leave me alone is because I said I wasn't interested. I think you like a challenge, but I can assure you, it's never going to happen."

"Hmm...." She tapped a pointed, blood-red nail against her chin. "I'm starting to get very curious about *why* it's never going to happen. You intrigue me, Rodie. One of these days I'm going to figure everything out. Have a good rest of the night, Sheriff."

I slammed the door shut once she was gone. I grabbed a handful of hair and pulled until it hurt. I hated nothing more than people prying into my business. It was even worse when they were doing it for the sole purpose of making my life difficult.

Grumbling out loud, I took a seat behind my desk. I leaned forward until my forehead touched the hardwood. That impending headache was now a full-fledged rager, making my vision slightly blurry and causing my entire skull to feel like it was trapped in a vise. Unfortunately, I still had a job to do, so I pushed through the pounding in my head and the hollow feeling in my gut. When I finished the reports and did a quick check of the night shift, it was well past midnight. I lived in a small, two-bedroom craftsman that wasn't too far from the station, but for some reason, when I got into my SUV to head home, the idea of walking into my empty, dark, lonely house made my heart hurt.

It'd been a bad day, and I didn't want to end it stuck in the vortex of negativity and darkness that I could practically feel swirling around the top of my head.

I didn't have Wyatt's phone number.

I knew how the man sounded when I sucked on the tip of his tongue, and how he reacted when I bit his bottom lip. I knew that his skin was both smooth and soft, rough and hard in certain spots. I knew his eyes went from a light, periwinkle blue to a stormy, dark navy when he was aroused. And I knew exactly which buttons to push in order to get him to react to me since I loathed the cool indifference he was so good at hiding behind.

How could all of those intimate details be stored away in my memory, yet I had no way to contact him? It was clear I was pretty much clueless and acting on instinct when it came to dealing with Wyatt Bryant.

Deciding not to question the desire, or the spontaneity to follow it, I wheeled the SUV around and headed out of town toward the Warner ranch. I didn't know if Wyatt would be up, or if he would be willing to see me, so it might be a wasted trip. It still seemed like a better option than sulking around my house in a dark mood. I always felt better when I was around Wyatt, and I wasn't in the mindset to question that.

I did send a text to Ten, knowing she was a light sleeper, letting her know I was driving out to the ranch so she could warn the others. The last thing I needed was Cyrus or Lane pulling a shotgun on me because I was showing up on their property in the middle of the night unannounced. Being the good friend she was, Ten didn't ask me why I was suddenly popping up so late, and she told me she wouldn't mention the late-night visit to Webb, which I appreciated. I wasn't sure if Wyatt's younger brother approved of my interest in his sibling, and there was already so much I was working around. I knew Webb's disapproval might be the last straw in any budding relationship.

I parked alongside the bunkhouse when I arrived. If I left it parked out front or up by the main house, rumors would fly around town about the sheriff being out at the Warner's in the middle of the night. People would make up stories to fit a dramatic narrative simply because that's what folks in small towns did. With all the attention and pressure the mayor was already putting on me, I didn't need to open the door to anymore gossip.

I knocked lightly on the door, not wanting to wake Wyatt if he was already asleep. Just the drive out to the ranch had helped clear some of the ugly thoughts swirling in my head, so I wasn't going to be too upset if it was a wasted trip.

It wasn't. Moments later, Wyatt pulled open the door. He was dressed the same as the last time I dropped by unexpectedly. He was wearing only a pair of low-riding sweatpants that left little to the imagination, and holding a beer in one hand. He was so pretty, even the places on his body that were a tell-tale reminder that his life had been anything but beautiful. His pale eyebrows shot nearly to his hairline as he stared at me in surprise.

"Rodie? Are you okay? What are you doing here at this time of night?" The concerned look on his face turned my heart over in my chest. It'd been a very long time since anyone was worried about my well-being.

I let my head drop because it honestly felt too heavy to hold up any longer. "I had a bad day."

I jolted slightly when Wyatt's hand shot out and landed on the side of my neck. His strong fingers dug into a particularly tense spot, and I almost melted at his bare feet.

"Come on in, Sheriff." He dropped his hand and motioned into the darkened interior of the room behind him. "Let's see if we can turn your day around."

I followed blindly, mouth going dry at the sight of his muscled back and the flex of his seriously perfect ass. In that moment, I was willing to risk a lot for this man — hell, risk it all — and at some point we were going to have to figure out if he was willing to risk anything for me.

CHAPTER 10

WYATT

H E LOOKED LIKE HE'D had a bad day. Not that Rodie was typically a smiley, cheerful kinda guy. Tonight, the strain around his pretty green eyes was evident, and the furrow between his burnished eyebrows was deep. He didn't have his hat on, and his coppery hair looked like he'd been running frustrated fingers through those silken strands for hours. It was against my better judgment to let him in this late while he was in an unpredictable mood, but I couldn't turn him away. I hadn't spoken to Rodie since our unexpected kiss in the front of his SUV, not that I was sure what I wanted to say. However, I did spend a good portion of the days that had passed since, wondering if he was obsessing and dissecting every single second our lips had touched the same way I had been. Now that there were no questions left about Rodie's sexuality, it was much harder to tell myself that he was off-limits and that he should remain that way.

I waved him toward the small table and asked him if he wanted a drink. He nodded, not bothering to offer up a beverage preference, so I got him a beer. I popped it open and set it on the table in front of him. I took a seat next to him and asked again, "What's wrong?"

Rather than answer right away, he reached out and fiddled with the tab on the can. His expression darkened by shades, and his mouth pulled into an angry, flat line. Irritated at the deafening silence, and uneasy with the level of tension snapping in the air around him, I grabbed his chin and forced him to look me in the eye. He was pretty cute when he was all sulky like this, but I still wanted to know what brought him to my door in the middle of the night. "Talk to me, Rodie."

After another minute, he finally sighed heavily and caught my hand in his, pulling it away from his face. He didn't let it go. Instead, his index finger started to randomly trace patterns across the back of it and down the length of my fingers. The absentminded caress made my breath catch in my chest and made other parts of my anatomy perk up with slowly seeping desire.

"I like my job. When I first ran for sheriff, it was such a long shot. I didn't really care if I got the position one way or the other, but then the people of Sheridan picked me, and suddenly being the sheriff meant a lot to me. It felt like I'd finally been accepted by the people who spent my entire childhood looking down on me. It was a ridiculous assumption on my part. I got the job because of my service record and because there wasn't a better option at the time. They never accepted me, but they tolerated me because they didn't have another choice. Over time I knew I could prove that I deserved the job, and I believe I have. It pisses me off that all that hard work, and all the years of trying to be who this town wants me to be, won't matter when they finally have options."

It was a slightly disjointed rant, but I could hear the concern and worry thick in his deep voice. I was smart enough to pick the important parts out of the rambling diatribe.

"They found someone to run against you for sheriff? And you're worried the town will vote for him instead of you when it's time for the election." I couldn't imagine anyone in a hundred-mile radius being more qualified for the position than

Rodie, so it seemed unlikely he would lose based on experience and qualifications alone, but I knew that was only part of what motivated small-town voters. I actually understood his worry. I knew when I finally woke up in the hospital with wires and tubes sticking out of me, my time as a field agent was over. Losing the career that defines you, the one that gave you purpose and drive, was unbelievably hard. Shifting the hold he had on my hand, I clasped our palms together and gave a comforting squeeze. "I don't think you need to worry about anything. You're clearly the right man for the job. I think you need to have a little more faith in yourself and the people you've served throughout the years."

"It doesn't matter. Nothing I've done, none of the accomplishments I achieved would mean shit if they knew the real me. Just look who they voted to be the mayor: an asshole who's openly a bigot." He sounded so angry and frustrated. I didn't enjoy watching Rodie struggle, and I was surprised at how badly I wanted to soothe him. I was normally more of a 'suck-it-up' kind of guy. He had a point, as much as I hated to admit it. The mayor was obviously homophobic, so it wasn't a stretch to imagine the rest of the town following his lead if he suddenly turned on Rodie. I couldn't begin to imagine the pressure he was under to keep up an unflappable front and hide who he really was for the sake of his career.

Looking down at our entwined hands, a rush of heat pushed through me. "Maybe it's time to consider going somewhere you don't have to hide who you really are. Instead of trying to force yourself to fit in, find a place where you actually do. I fully believe you are an excellent law enforcement officer, and if the people of Sheridan can't see that, then they don't deserve you."

Our eyes locked when I finished my rant, and suddenly a different kind of tension was thick in the air between us. We watched each other silently for a long, drawn-out moment. Our breathing was loud in the quiet space, so was my heartbeat. I wondered if he could hear it. I wondered if he could see the way I reacted to him, even though I didn't want to. He was the last person I planned on having a crush on. After all, I was a grown-ass man and should have better control over my emotions at this point in my life. But I was having a hard time shaking these feelings off.

In the blink of an eye, I was suddenly pulled from my seat and sprawled across Rodie's rock hard thighs in an ungraceful heap as he positioned me on his lap. While I was unsteady, he used his hold on my hand and my own unpredictable balance against me. I ended up straddling him and was almost close enough that the tips of our noses touched. My first instinct was to fight my way free of the arms wrapped tightly around me to keep me in place. I wasn't a small guy, even in my battered state. I wasn't used to being manhandled and pulled around by whomever I let get close enough to put their hands on me. I was the one in charge, usually. I was the one who called the shots.

But not with Rodie.

For whatever reason, I let him lead, and I happily followed. It was the opposite of my personality, and I couldn't figure out what it was about him that made me act so differently.

I put one of my hands on the center of his chest to get some space between us. The strong muscles in his thighs weren't the only hard part of his body I was currently pressed against. There was no ignoring the way our proximity affected him, and if he didn't let me pull back, the thin material of my sweatpants was going to reveal that I reacted the exact same way. And if I shifted, just slightly, the hardness I was trying so hard to dismiss was going to be pressed intimately against Rodie's hardness, which was impossible to ignore.

"What about you, Wyatt?" One of his eyebrows danced upward, and finally the frown on his face lifted. He gave me a lopsided grin that sent shivers racing up and down my spine.

I hadn't bothered to put on a shirt and was suddenly acutely aware of his rough hands on the exposed skin of my back. A shot of insecurity made me double my efforts to put some distance between us. "Do you deserve me?"

He had called me pretty at the airport, and when he dropped me off at Miranda's the other day, but I was currently anything but. I hadn't planned on anyone seeing the wear and tear on my body up close and personal for a long time. I needed to prepare myself mentally for that kind of silent judgment.

Only, there was nothing but appreciation in Rodie's green gaze as his eyes raked over the flexing muscles in my arms and chest. He asked if I deserved him, but I didn't have an answer. I still had no clue if he was a good idea, or the worst one I'd ever had. Fortunately, Rodie didn't seem interested in getting a reply.

One of his hands lifted and landed on the back of my head. He pulled me down until our lips lined up. This kiss was softer, less frantic and harsh than our first, but no less memorable. Instead of being in a rush and worrying about being caught, he took his time, savoring every slide and slip of our tongues as they rubbed against one another. This kiss wasn't stolen. It wasn't a surprise. It was sweet and slow, and all too easy to sink into.

The hand I had rested on his chest curled around the back of his neck as I unconsciously pulled him closer. He made a sound of satisfaction as one of his palms skated down the length of my spine. My cock throbbed in response, and I no longer worried about keeping my reaction to him in check. I could feel the heat and hardness behind his zipper pressing insistently against the inside of my thigh. I wanted closer. I wanted more.

I wanted him.

I let out a startled sound when he abruptly stood, taking me with him. I jerked my mouth away from his to protest, but I never got the chance. He dropped me with a soft *thump* onto the top of the wooden table and immediately stepped between my spread legs. I didn't even care that both of the beer cans went tumbling to the floor. He leaned over me, using his broad shoulders and intense stare to guide me backward. Before I could pull my wits together and get my mind off my throbbing dick, he was hovering over me, pinning me down as he watched me with a wolfish smile and glittering eyes.

He braced himself over me with a forearm curled above my head, as his other hand started to leisurely trail over my chest. His fingers were surprisingly gentle whenever they encountered a scar, old or new. Apparently, he not only wanted to seduce, he wanted to soothe, as well.

Before I could get completely caught up in the moment, I asked, "You're the one in a bad mood. Shouldn't I do something to make you feel better?" I wasn't ignorant of where things had been headed the moment I let him in the door. I was surprised that instead of letting me distract him, he was doing his best to keep me off balance and wound up.

"If you don't think seeing you like this, getting to touch you like this, doesn't instantly make me feel better, you haven't been paying attention." His warm lips dragged across the ridge of my cheekbone and down across my jaw. I bit back a moan when I felt the edge of his teeth on the side of my neck. I liked that he didn't treat me as if I was going to break any second. I was so tired of feeling broken and fragile, it was nice to be treated normally by someone. I wanted to be seen as desirable, as something more than a burden.

What was happening between the two of us might boil down to the need for a distraction from the building complications in our lives, but what a distraction it was.

My abs tightened almost painfully when one of Rodie's thumbs brushed lightly over my nipple. His fingers purposefully traced a path downward, as his mouth moved along my neck, then up to my ear. When I felt the nip of his teeth on my earlobe any remaining resistance drifted away.

I arched into his touch as his fingers outlined the muscles of my stomach, tracing the carved indents that arrowed sharply down into the soft fabric of the sweats. I was glad I hadn't lost most of the definition in my abs since he seemed to appreciate how the hours of hard work had paid off.

When his fingers hit the fine, pale trail of blond hair that disappeared into the waistband of my pants, I put my hands to work trying to wrestle him out of his ugly uniform shirt. I was in decent shape, but I had nothing on him. I could tell whenever we were pressed closely together how strong he was. I could see it when he moved a certain way and all those muscles strained against the seams of his clothes. He was taller than I was, bigger, but in no way did he make me feel delicate or small in comparison. I liked that he didn't try and rein in his strength when he handled me.

I must've been more eager and impatient than I thought. Buttons popped and hit the wood floors with tiny pings. Rodie chuckled against my skin as my seeking hands finally found bare skin. He had tale-tell patches that were lifted and smooth, scattered across his shoulders and torso, much like I did. There a light dusting of freckles on his collarbone, making me wonder if he'd been more of a redhead than he was now back in his youth. His skin tone was lighter than mine, but he had an attractive patch of burnished chest hair, where I was smooth. We both appeared to appreciate the fine art of manscaping, but I was right about his body being something close to perfection.

He looked like one of those ancient Greek statues carved out of marble, pale and perfect, even with the scars and marks littered all over him. I couldn't remember a single time I'd been with anyone who understood what it was like to have the body of a survivor. I never dated anyone in my field because it was easier that way. Every single time things progressed to the point where clothes started coming off, I had to issue warnings and explanations. It was eye-opening to be with someone who simply *knew*. With Rodie, there was a sense of relief, a sense of rightness I'd never felt before.

The instant his hand slipped past the barrier of my pants, I felt like an electrical current shot through me. His palm was warm and sure when it wrapped around the pulsing length of my cock. It felt like my brain short-circuited. The entire world narrowed to the places on my body where Rodie was touching me, where he was tasting me.

His mouth slid over mine as his hand started a steady glide up and down the rigid length between my legs. I could feel his cock straining, pressing against my leg, and I wanted desperately to get my hands on it, but he kept me pinned beneath him as he manhandled me into submission. I swore against his questing mouth, and felt him smile in response. He knew he was driving me out of my mind, and he loved every second of the control he had over me.

My shoulders came off the table when his thumb skillfully slipped over the damp head of my cock. There was already moisture leaking from the slit, and Rodie's gaze turned absolutely predatory when he pulled that kind of response from me. His kiss turned dangerous and demanding as he shifted to pull the stretchy material of my sweats out of the way. My cock immediately stood upright. The sight was erotic and undeniably sexy as Rodie's hand wrapped back around it.

I moved restlessly underneath him as his mouth lifted from mine and moved to the center of my chest. I felt like I was going to go up in flames everywhere his mouth touched. I muttered his name and slid my fingers through his thick hair. I felt him smile as I held his head, guiding it lower. Anticipation tightened my entire body, and I'm pretty sure I forgot how to breathe for a minute.

"Pretty." Rodie rasped the word against my lower abdomen. I would've been insulted if it was anyone else, but I knew he really did think I was pretty, even in my tattered state. There was a level of reassurance in that single word that I had no idea I needed.

A moment later his mouth replaced his hand on my overly eager dick and I couldn't stop a long, loud moan from pouring out of my mouth. The heat and wetness surrounding my hard flesh was everything. His hand most certainly felt good, his mouth was unbelievably better. It was the best.

He swirled his tongue in such a way that spots of white exploded behind my eyelids. My back arched, and my hands pulled relentlessly at his hair. My hips lifted, chasing pleasure and his warm mouth, as Rodie took me apart with every flick of his tongue and every precise and practiced suck. I wasn't sure if anyone had ever handled me this well, this thoroughly. If they had, their memory was about to be replaced because I was never going to forget how well and how quickly he learned what I liked.

When the tip of his tongue slid across the slippery slit, picking up the drops of fluid there, I knew I wasn't going to last much longer. I'd been alone and on the mend for a long time. I already had a hair trigger, and considering he'd been the star in all of my most recent fantasies, there was no holding out against his skilled ministrations. He was like a symphony conductor, expertly making my body play the tune he wanted.

I pried my eyes open, and our gazes locked with an intensity I wasn't prepared for.

The way he was looking at me, the absolute appreciation in those green eyes, was all it took to push me over the edge. I didn't even have the chance to warn Rodie. Between one gasp and another, I exploded in a rush of pleasure and nearly pulled out a handful of his hair in my lust-induced euphoria.

I heard him swallow reflexively, then chuckle as he pulled away from my happily satiated dick. He sat up, dragged the back of his hand across his mouth, and looked at me with a lifted eyebrow. Part of me wanted to wipe that cocky, satisfied smile off his face, but a bigger part of me realized he deserved it. There was no denying he was as good at giving head as he was at everything else.

I swore, throwing an arm over my eyes as he rose to his feet.

"Gotta say, I ended this crap day on a high note. You know how to make a man smile, Special Agent." I jolted when he caught one of my nipples between his fingers and gave it a tug. "Thanks for letting me in tonight, Wyatt."

I knew he was getting ready to say goodbye, so I bolted upright and reached for him. I caught one of his elbows and told him, "Don't go." I was going to have to get creative with my physical limitations, because there was no way I was getting back up if I got down on my knees, but I wanted, no *needed*, to return the favor.

Rodie gave me a considering look and asked, "You sure you want me to stay?"

I nodded, holding out a hand so he could help me off the table. "I'm sure."

I didn't know much of anything at the moment when it came to my life. But I knew without question, I wasn't finished with Rodie Collins in any way, shape, or form.

CHAPTER 11

RODIE

"SORRY I'M LATE." I pulled my hat off and slid into the booth across from Miranda. We hadn't been able to make a dinner date work, but I offered to buy her breakfast before work the last time we chatted. I didn't know I would be driving in from the Warner Ranch, or that I would be reluctant to leave the bed that had a very naked Wyatt Bryant in it. I couldn't remember the last time I'd spent the night sleeping next to someone. I'd forgotten how nice it was to sleep skin to skin and how sweet the sound of someone else's soft breathing could be. I would've stayed in that spot next to him forever if it was an option.

Miranda gave me one of her sad smiles as she looked at me over the top of her menu. "Are you actually sorry?"

I chuckled because she knew me so well. "No. What I was doing was worth being a little late."

Wyatt might not be able to bend and move fluidly, but he was creative, and when he wanted something, there wasn't much that could stop him from getting it. I took a lot of pride in being able to satisfy my partner, but so did he. I'd had a feeling when all of his intensity and focus was directed at something pleasurable, it would be devastating, and I was right. For the first time in forever, I felt like I very well might have met my match. So even though I was late and it was early in the morning after a night of little sleep, I was still smiling and remembering all the ways Wyatt used his hands and mouth on my very willing body.

Miranda set down the menu and tilted her head to the side as she considered me silently for a moment. "You look happy, Rhodes. I wasn't sure what was different about you when you brought your special agent in to see me, but now I know. I don't think I've ever seen you look this way."

I picked up a menu, even though I knew what was offered by heart. This diner was close to the sheriff's office and the only restaurant open late in Sheridan. I ate here once or twice a week and knew almost all of the waitstaff by name.

"It's been a long time since you've looked this way, Miranda." I gave her a pointed look. "You deserve to be happy more than anyone I know."

We both looked up as the waitress stopped at the edge of the table, dropping off two steaming mugs of coffee. With a sleepy smile, she asked if I wanted my regular order and if Miranda was ready to place hers. Once we were alone again, I put my forearms on the table and leaned toward my longtime friend and advocate.

"Do you ever think about leaving Sheridan and starting over somewhere else?" When Wyatt asked why I stayed somewhere I'd never felt like I didn't belong, I had a hard time coming up with a good reason why. The only thing I could think of was that Sheridan was my hometown and I knew what to expect day in and day out. After a career spent in warzones, and never knowing if this day would be my last, the predictability was nice.

Miranda wrapped her small hands around her mug and watched me over the rim as she took a sip. She made a face and pulled her gaze away from mine. "Where would I go?" She sighed and tapped her nails on the side of the mug. "I'm too old to start over."

I shook my head in automatic denial. "No, you're not. What you are is too young to give up and accept that this sadness and emptiness is all there is to your life. You can find someone to make you smile again. You can find a new version of happiness, Miranda." All she had to do was put the work in.

She made a sound and blinked wide eyes at me. "I think you're oversimplifying things. Not all of us are so lucky to have a smoking hot special agent fall into our laps. Think about it, if Wyatt wasn't injured, he never would have found himself recovering here. You met him before he was hurt and never made a move because you knew he was going back to Washington. Are you telling me you would've chased after the man? Do you think he would have let you catch him when he was able to run away?"

I did my best not to flinch at her insightful observation. I'd wanted Wyatt from the start, but I hadn't done anything about it because he was going to leave, and I knew that I wasn't going anywhere. It seemed impossible until Wyatt got injured and ended up back in Wyoming. I wasn't about to let my chance pass me by, but Miranda had a point. If he disappeared tomorrow, there was a good chance I wasn't going after him.

I cleared my throat a little louder than necessary and picked up my own mug. "We're talking about you, not me. I know you loved Abe more than anything and losing him is not something you'll ever fully get over. But you have one of the biggest hearts I've ever seen. I know you have more love to give." Abe Connelly had saved my life on more than one occasion, and I credited him for making me into a man I could be proud of most of the time. I still wasn't over my former CO's death, and struggled with it daily, wondering if there was more I could've done to prevent what happened with him.

Losing someone you loved was never easy, but when you lost someone to suicide, there were so many more questions and lingering regrets wrapped up in the grief. It was a tangled web that was difficult to fight through. And just when you thought you were free and clear, fine, gossamer tendrils would cling to you in the form of memories, reminding you the loss was always there, the hole the person left in your heart was never fully filled.

"I still miss him every day," I told her quietly.

That heartbreaking smile tugged at her mouth. She reached across the table and put one of her hands over mine. "I know you do." She sighed slightly, and blinked eyes that were suddenly teary. "I won't leave because he's still here. I feel him in our home, in the land he loved. I'll never forget how excited he was when I agreed to his crazy plan to move to Wyoming and become a cowboy." She let out a strained laugh and pulled back to shyly wipe at her eyes. "I hated you before I got the chance to know you. I don't know if I ever told you that."

I gave her a shocked look and leaned back in the booth. "What!?" Miranda was key in my recovery. She was the only loving, maternal figure I'd ever had in my life. She had gone above and beyond nursing me back to health, and we'd held each other together when my CO was no longer around to do it for us. She was never anything other than loving and kind to me.

She laughed again, but this time there was a spark of humor in her gaze. "When Abe told me he wanted to uproot our entire life and move to some place in Wyoming I'd never heard of, I thought he'd lost his mind. I knew he was burned out mentally and physically from his career in the military, but I guess I never realized just how exhausted he was. He went on and on about this place and the kid who came from here. He admired you so much. You really were like the son he never had. I was convinced he never would've had such a wild idea if it hadn't been for you." She playfully narrowed her eyes at me and pointed a finger at the end of my nose. "I spent my first Wyoming winter cursing you out in every way imaginable."

Winter in Wyoming was on a different level. The cold was brutal. The landscape empty and barren. During the summer, Sheridan was an outdoor lover's dream and the state's economy thrived on tourism. In the winter, this place was like something out of an apocalypse. The wind was enough to strip the skin from your bones, and bitter cold made it almost impossible to go outside. I didn't blame her for not wanting to suffer through that year after year, but I knew she did so willingly because of her love for the man who'd been like a father to me.

I started to apologize, to tell her that I had no clue I was influencing my former CO when I talked about home, but she quickly shushed me and waved off the words.

"As soon as we settled in, Abe was at peace. I think moving here gave me more time with him. I knew he was unhappy when he retired, but I didn't know how deep that depression ran. It went away for a while when we came here, but started to seep back in slowly. It seemed to fade again when he brought you home and was focused on helping you heal, but once you were back on your feet, I could tell he was sinking into the darkness again. I always wanted forever with Abe, but deep down, I knew I was only going to get him for a short amount of time. I love that this place let me keep him with me a little longer, so I don't think I'll be going anywhere anytime soon. You, on the other hand," her eyebrows danced upwards knowingly, "This place takes and takes from you and has yet to give much back in return. I've never understood why you seem so determined to stay."

Wyatt's words telling me I deserved better rang in my ears.

When I was younger, I honestly believed I deserved the poor treatment and I got everywhere I went. I thought the judgment was normal and that I'd never really done anything to earn the acceptance and respect I so desperately wanted. I knew better now. I'd done nothing wrong back then, and neither had my mother. It made no sense that I was now literally back at the very beginning of my life, trying to fit in and belong, while risking my life for people who didn't give a damn about me.

"The mayor found someone to run against me in the upcoming election, and his assistant is trying to blackmail me into having an affair with her." I bit the words out. Furious just thinking about the stupid game I was caught in.

The waitress popped back up at the edge of the table, placed our breakfast in front of us, and asked if we needed anything else. Miranda politely sent her on her way, leaning over the food-laden plate with huge eyes.

"What are you going to do about both of those things? Is there someone you can report them to?"

I snorted and stabbed a sausage angrily with my fork. "I could report her for sexual harassment, not that anyone would believe me. But our esteemed mayor is not technically doing anything wrong." The sarcasm couldn't be any thicker in my tone.

Her brow furrowed as she ignored her food and started to worry in earnest about my situation. "You're worried about them finding out about you. Even more so, now that Special Agent Bryant is in the picture."

I sighed heavily and dipped my chin in a slight nod. "I knew I couldn't keep it a secret forever, but I wanted to be able to decide when and with whom I talked about it. I don't like having my hand forced, especially by a homophobic prick and his lecherous assistant."

She nodded solemnly in agreement. "You don't owe anyone any kind of explanation about your private life. Not even the people in this town who voted for you. Wyatt doesn't seem like the overly flashy type, and he's mentioned more than once he's unsure how long he's staying in Sheridan. Maybe you're worrying about the unknowns for nothing."

I stabbed another link on my plate with more force than necessary. "Wyatt doesn't give a shit what anyone thinks. He kept his personal business to himself when he was working with the DEA, but he doesn't hide anything. He's a fierce advocate for anyone he sees being wronged for being perceived as different." He was a fighter. It was one of the things I liked most about him. It was something I desperately envied. I wanted the freedom to speak on things I considered wrong, but I always let fear hold me back.

Miranda picked absently at her pile of French toast. "He's going to bring your carefully built house of cards down around you, Rhodes." I couldn't tell if she sounded pleased by the fact, or if she was trying to warn me. If I was being honest, a small part of me was pleased about the chaos that Wyatt could rain down upon this town.

"I know he is." But there was nothing I could do about it. At the end of the day, I wanted him more than I wanted to keep pretending to be someone I wasn't.

Finally, Miranda smiled. A real, happy smile full of love and light. "I'm so glad he ended up here. There have been moments since I've met you that I worried you and Abe were headed in the same direction. No one can live their entire life denying who they are without it taking a serious toll. If Wyatt is the catalyst that finally pushes you to be honest with yourself and what you want, then I owe him more than I can say. He's going to save your life, Rodie."

I didn't think it was that serious, but I could admit he was making me re-evaluate the way I'd been living.

I gave her a grin and told her, "Maybe I'm going to save his."

That glowing smile dimmed some, and the familiar heartbreak crept back into her gaze. "That's what love is. Recognizing what each other needs and saving one another whenever you need saving."

I knew without asking she was once again thinking of Abe and how he'd slipped away from us. I tried to change the subject to something lighter because I didn't want to go back there when we'd both spent too much time trying to learn to live with the constant hurt.

"Speaking of Wyatt, how's he doing with physical therapy?" I knew he'd been going into town to see her a few times a week.

"Good. Like you said, he's a fighter. He's in good shape and excellent health already, which helps. He gets frustrated with himself easily and wants results faster than he's seeing them, but I think we're in a good place and on the right track. If he keeps up with the exercises I've taught him and works on stretching, I predict he'll be able to maneuver without the cane within six months, give or take a few."

He maneuvered without it just fine when we were in bed together, but she didn't need to know that. I bit back a grin and muttered, "Good to know." I didn't mind getting on my knees for him, but he mentioned he wanted to return the favor when he was able, and he couldn't at the moment without pain. I was pretty easygoing when it came to sex. I liked it in all forms and positions. I rolled with the mood, and Wyatt was the same. I was surprised, thinking he'd be a stickler and stuck in one role or the other, but the man was far less uptight when he was naked than I thought he'd be. He didn't even argue when I barked orders at him and demanded he let me heap attention and pleasure on his willing body. I wasn't ready for the quiet submission, but it did almost as much to undo me as his mouth around my cock. We just kept finding out we were more and more compatible every minute we spent together.

We kept the conversation playful and light as we finished breakfast. We were arguing over who was going to pay the bill when my cell phone rang. I went on alert when I recognized the number from my office on the display. I wasn't on duty yet, so I didn't bring my radio, but all my deputies had my number in case of an emergency. Seeing the expression on my face as I answered the call, Miranda gave me a silent goodbye, slipping out of the booth with the bill.

"There's a problem at the high school." The deputy sounded worried, and I didn't blame him. We rarely got calls from the school, and this was the second one within a month.

"Don't tell me the mayor's kid is involved again." I knew I wasn't going to get that lucky.

A heavy sigh came over the line. "No can do, boss. It's him and the same kid from last time. The mayor's already up there raising hell. It sounds like it's about to get ugly."

"Son of a bitch," I uttered a few more choice words under my breath as I hurried out of the diner toward my SUV. "I'm on my way."

I knew this wasn't going to be good, and I couldn't help the slight surge of panic shooting through my blood at the thought of something bad happening to Cam. I would've been him if I'd been more honest and open when I was younger. I couldn't stop a trickle of worry over what this situation was going to mean for me and Wyatt, because I knew without a doubt that Cam wasn't going to be facing the mayor and his bully of a son alone.

CHAPTER 12

WYATT

IT TOOK BOTH ME and Brynn to hold Lane back in the principal's tiny office. The youngest Warner looked like he was ready to take the mayor's head off, and if we let him go, there was a high probability of that happening. The mayor seemed unfazed in the face of the cowboy's ire, mostly because he was cowering in front of the oldest Warner. There was simply something about Cyrus Warner that demanded immediate respect. While the mayor was still mouthy and defiant when he spoke, he was less blustery in the face of someone who naturally held the kind of authority he'd sought by being an elected official. The mayor wanted to use his title and position to get his own way. Cy didn't need either of those things to command all the attention in the room. I'd never seen anything like it. Even when I used to have a badge to flash at people, I never got instant respect and admiration the way Cy did. It was impressive as hell.

The principal looked frazzled and on the verge of losing his breakfast. He was pale and sweaty, his nervous gaze darting between the two sullen teenage boys caught in the middle of the war being waged by the adults.

Cam was holding an ice pack to his mouth and had a wide bandage secured to his forehead. This time, the mayor's kid was the one who looked like the victor. According to Cam, Dalton had been goading him, prodding him, and picking on him for weeks following their last dust-up. When Cam couldn't take it any longer, he'd lashed out, only Dalton was waiting for the day Cam was pushed too far. It wasn't just the mayor's dirt-bag of a son waiting for Cam to lose his temper and attack. It'd been Dalton and four of his friends. When the fight broke out in the gymnasium, all hell broke loose. Cam was lucky he only had a split lip and gash on his head. Being ganged up on like that, beaten from every direction, could've led to something so much worse. I didn't blame Lane for breathing fire and wanting the principal's and the mayor's heads on a pike.

"Again, Cam admits he's the one who instigated the fight. We have multiple witnesses who corroborate the fact. School policy means he has to be expelled." The principal wrung his hands together nervously when Cyrus switched his intent stare over to him as he spoke.

"What was done the multiple times Cameron complained to you about the ongoing harassment he was receiving from this young man and his friends? Did you file a report? Did you take any preventive actions? Or have you been complicit, forcing Cam to take his safety and well-being into his own hands?" Cy never raised his voice or postured to make himself look more intimidating. He simply asked the questions and watched every single move the principal made, judging.

"We followed all of the proper procedures when handling Cam's complaints. There was no evidence to support his complaints of harassment. Dalton has a crystal-clear school record. He's been a model student since elementary school. The accusations are outrageous."

A low, rumbling growl came from Cy's chest, and Lane jerked so hard he shook loose of the hold I had on him. Lane and Cy stood shoulder to shoulder, making the principal cower and forcing the mayor to fall back a step.

"So, what you're saying is that because Dalton has been in the school system longer than Cam, school policy is going to favor him?" Lane bit out the words, each one angrier than the one before. "Doesn't seem right."

I cleared my throat from where I was leaning against the wall at Cam's side. The kid had been quiet, but I could tell his spirit was hurting, and that he was just as frustrated as his guardian.

I rubbed my thumb against the corner of my mouth and waited until I had both the principal's and mayor's eyes on me. "Doesn't matter what the school policy is, if this institution is going to discriminate against Cam because of his sexuality, we're going to get a human rights lawyer involved. I'll have all your names in the press, and make sure what you're doing here goes public, far and wide. Your job is to protect *all* students, not just the ones you've known since elementary school. You're preventing Cam from getting the same education as everyone else because of your own prejudice." And there was no way I was going to stay still and let that happen.

"You again? Why are you even here?" The mayor glared at me, putting a protective hand on his son's shoulder.

I lifted a challenging eyebrow. "I'm here because, just like Cam, I'm an outsider. I didn't grow up in this town. I'm not willing to accept the excuse that just because things have always been one way for so long, that's how they should stay. It's not an acceptable reason for bad behavior. I know how the world works outside the fishbowl of Sheridan. I don't have a business and reputation to protect in this town, so I've got nothing to lose when it comes to keeping this kid safe and making sure he's treated fairly." I shot Cam a look out of the corner of my eye and asked, "Are you sure you don't need a doctor? I want to make sure you get your head checked out. You might have a concussion." If he did, I was going to encourage the Warners to drag the school through the very dirty legal mud for their lack of action.

Brynn wrapped her arm around Cam's shoulder and dropped a kiss on his uninjured temple. "I'm so sorry you're going through this." Her voice was soft and comforting, but there was a thread of steel running through it. She wasn't about to let this corrupt system mess with her baby either.

Cam tried to smile, but winced when the movement pulled at his battered mouth. "Been through worse."

I heard Brynn's teeth click together and grind as she furiously whispered, "But I promised you it would all be behind you. I'm so angry right now."

I inclined my head toward the door, "Take him to the ER to get checked out. Make sure they take a close look at his head."

Brynn nodded and started to usher the teenager out of the hostile room. Everyone paused when the mayor suddenly burst out, "Where do you think you're going? I called the sheriff. We're pressing charges. That little fairy is going to jail for assault."

My spine stiffened and I heard Brynn gasp. Cy let out a string of swear words, and Lane once again lunged for the mayor, but was brought up short by his older brother's arm.

I put my hand on Brynn's back and urged her toward the door. "Don't worry about that. If Sheriff Collins needs to talk to Cam later, he can come find him at the hospital or at home. It's illegal to deny an injured person medical attention during an investigation." The law was a little gray in that area, but I doubted any of the people in this room knew the finer details, and I wanted Cam gone before Rodie showed up. This situation was about to go from bad to worse, very quickly, once Rodie walked through the doors.

The mayor huffed and puffed as Brynn led the shaken teenager out of the room, but no one was daring enough to take on Cy or Lane to get their hands on the boy. I scowled when I realized the mayor's son was smirking and watching the fallout of his actions with unabashed pride.

When our eyes met, I asked the other kid, "Proud of yourself?"

He shrugged, but there was no mistaking the boastful gleam in his beady eyes.

I gave him a grin that was sharp and asked, "Knew you would get your ass kicked if you tried to take him on one-on-one again, so you ganged up on him, didn't you? That's about the most cowardly thing I've ever heard. Four on one. You're all lucky Cam is still breathing after that. No wonder you hide behind your daddy every time you get in trouble. Sounds like he never taught you to stand on your own two feet."

"Hey, fuck you!" The teenager tried to lunge at me, but was halted by his father and the principal.

"Enough." The principal held up his hand and cleared his throat. "Regardless of Cam's personal life, policy is policy and there is no arguing he started this fight. Whatever legal ramifications may or may not follow have nothing to do with the school." The older man rubbed a hand down his face and sighed in frustration. "I have to say, this is the first time we're facing these kinds of issues in our school district, and Cam joining our school is the only thing that's changed recently."

"Cam is not the problem," Lane growled the words, still straining against Cy's hold. "Your inaction and prejudice are to blame here."

"Ahhh... Sheriff Collins, finally." The mayor puffed up his chest. "My son was assaulted and I want to press charges. I know you will make sure justice is served."

Rodie had a stern, serious expression on his handsome face as he entered the room. His sharp gaze drifted over the occupants gathered, skimming over the mayor and his son, as well as the Warners. I felt it linger when it reached me, and I could see him stiffen. Our eyes locked for a brief second, and I had to remind myself this wasn't the same guy whose cock I'd sucked half the night. No, this was the sheriff of Sheridan, a man denying who he was, one who would put his job before anything, even the well-being of a scared kid. That realization had me holding my breath.

"Dalton and his buddies have been harassing Cam nonstop. He complained to the administration, but they've done nothing. Dalton cornered Cam in gym class and provoked him into starting something. Cam pushed Dalton, but then Dalton and his friends mobbed Cam. He was on the ground, being kicked and hit by four other kids when the teachers finally intervened." Lane laid out Cam's account of the events in a flat tone.

The tension in the room was thick enough to cut with a knife.

"That's bullshit. All I was doing was getting ready to ask Cam a question about homework when he suddenly went crazy and attacked me. There's something wrong with that kid. He's dangerous. He doesn't belong at this school." Defiantly, the teen crossed his arms over his chest and glared at all the adults in the room.

The mayor cleared his throat and tried to put on an authoritative expression. I thought he looked like he was constipated. "This is the second time he's put my son in danger. I'm worried about the safety of the students. I want something done about this, Sheriff."

Both Lane and Cy turned to look at Rodie. When Cy and the sheriff faced off, it was like the Clash of the Titans. Two big men with a lot of force and personality taking up all the available space and air. It was like two major stormfronts about to collide. I was moving before I was aware my feet were in motion. I stopped next to Rodie, tilting my head back slightly to meet his intense gaze.

"Cam was kicked in the head. We're worried he might have a concussion. Brynn took him to the hospital. One of your deputies is in the gym interviewing the witnesses and the teachers. It sounds like Cam did engage first, but he was provoked." I knew I wouldn't be able to ultimately sway him if he felt like there was enough there to charge Cam with something, but I needed him to know that Cam wouldn't act out without reason. I needed him to remember we'd both been in the same situation as Cam when we were younger, and neither one of us had been as brave and honest as he was.

"I know that Cam's been getting harassed by Dalton and his friends since the last time we were in this very office." Rodie's voice was low and almost scary.

The mayor puffed up, scowling at the sheriff. "What do you mean?"

"I asked my deputies who patrol the school to keep an eye on the situation. They've been monitoring Dalton and his friends interacting with Cam. They've mentioned that it seems like there is a group of boys constantly ganging up on Cam and giving him a hard time. I also asked Cam about the situation directly. He told me he complained to the school and nothing was being done, so I told him to make sure he was documenting everything. I'm sure once I talk to Cam, he'll have some sort of video or recording of what Dalton and his friends have been subjecting him to, at my suggestion to preserve evidence, of course. Did you know it's against school policy for anyone to use derogatory words and statements and openly threaten another student?" Rodie glared at the principal. "I checked with the district superintendent on my way over here, in case you were wondering."

Dalton balked and leaned back against his father. "This is a set-up. Whose side are you on?" He looked over his shoulder at his dad and whined, "I didn't do anything wrong."

"Quiet, Dalton." The mayor glared at Rodie, teeth grinding so loudly we could all hear them. "I'm curious, as well. Why exactly are you so concerned about this kid, Sheriff? What kind of relationship do you have with him?" He turned to look at Lane with a sneer. "Maybe you should be worrying about that runaway being taken advantage of by someone older in a position of authority."

I heard a low rumble escape Rodie's chest and reached out to put a hand on his arm. I immediately jerked it away when he turned burning eyes in my direction.

Seeing he'd finally scored a direct hit, the mayor straightened his shoulders and declared, "We're pressing charges regardless. He started the fight and that's against school policy."

Cy rolled his eyes as he turned toward the principal. "If you're expelling Cam for the fight, you better plan on expelling Dalton and the other instigators for the threats and language."

The principal held up both his hands in a gesture of surrender. "Fine. Fine. All of the boys involved will be punished properly. I'm warning everyone in this room, if Dalton and Cam can't figure out a way to get along, and if they keep disrupting the other students, both boys will be removed from the school on a permanent basis."

Lane made a sound of disbelief. The mayor and his son started to argue, but Rodie held up a hand and demanded everyone to be quiet.

"You need to do your job. It's your responsibility to follow up when a student tells you they feel threatened. As I already mentioned, I spoke with your boss on my way over here. He's now very aware of just how badly you've dropped the ball."

The principal swore quietly as the mayor hauled Dalton out of the room, giving Rodie a dirty look as he went. The animosity between the two city leaders was evident, and I knew whatever grudge the mayor had against Rodie had just been bumped up a notch.

"You're arresting my kid over my dead body, Rodie." Lane stepped into Rodie's space, putting a finger in his face.

"Calm down." I gently pushed Lane back, unconsciously taking Rodie's side in the argument I knew was coming. "You have to let him do his job."

"Last time we did that, he put my innocent brother in jail." Lane was heated and not thinking straight. He was never going to be able to think rationally when it came to the teen he thought of as his own.

"Let's go check on Cam and Brynn. We'll get him a lawyer, just in case." Cy's voice was calm, but he didn't look any happier than Lane. "I'd tell you it's nice to see you, Sheriff, but it hasn't been lately."

Rodie heaved a deep sigh. "Got a job to do. That's all there is to it. Keep Cam safe. Keep him away from Dalton and the mayor before things get even more out of hand."

Cy looked at me and cocked his head slightly. "You coming with us?"

I'd ridden into town with Brynn and still needed to find my way to either the hospital or the ranch. I nodded slowly, keeping my gaze on Rodie. "Yeah. Just give me a second."

The brothers exited the room, making it slightly easier to breathe. The principal muttered something about needing to get some air, leaving me and Rodie alone in the office. Wordlessly, we turned to face one another. I didn't want the man I'd slept next to last night to be the same one responsible for persecuting a kid who'd already had a terrible life full of rejection and judgment.

"You know things are going to get progressively worse for Cam; that's why you had your guys keeping an eye on him and warned him to document everything. He's going to end up dead if things keep going the way they are now." I shook my head. "You don't know what it's like to have to fight just because you exist." It was a low dig, but one that was true, nonetheless. "You have no clue how hard Cam has it." Or how difficult things had been for me for my entire youth. Sometimes I wished I'd pretended, played straight the way he had, but at the end of the day, I wanted to be free to be myself even if it made my life harder. It was ridiculous to weaponize love, and I refused to live that way.

"I don't know what Cam's going through, but I know exactly what the rest of these kids are capable of because I was one of them. I'm trying to keep him safe. I want to help him protect himself, but I still have to follow protocol. I need to talk to my deputy, then Cam. If there's enough evidence it was assault, I'll do what I have to do."

He was so cold, so matter-of-fact about it all, but I knew deep down inside he had to be hurting. All of this happening with Cam had to hit just a little too close to home for him, the same way it did for me.

I sighed, grabbing his shoulder and giving it a squeeze now that we were alone and there was no risk of anyone seeing the slight contact. "You better watch your back, Sheriff. It's one thing to have the mayor gunning for you, if you end up with the Warners as enemies, losing your job is going to be the least of your problems."

He paused, then nodded, shifting so my hand fell away. I watched him walk out of the room, shaking my head. I wasn't sure what was worse, having a crush on him when I thought he was a cute straight boy, or having a crush on him now, knowing he was a cute but very confused gay boy.

Once again, I wondered if I even liked him, because at the moment, it felt like I could very easily hate him.

CHAPTER 13

RODIE

I WASN'T SURE WYATT WAS going to let me in when I once again knocked on his door in the middle of the night. There was no hiding the disappointment in his gaze when he walked away from me earlier in the day. It mirrored the disappointment in Cam's gaze when I finally made it to the hospital to speak to him. The poor kid was at such a huge turning point in his life, thought he was leaving hate and prejudice behind him, only to end up smack-dab in the center of a new nightmare. He seemed resigned to the fact he was never going to find peace, and I could feel Brynn glaring daggers into my back as I offered useless platitudes. Nothing I could say was going to change the way the mayor's son had been raised or shine a light on the darkness in a prejudiced heart. I'd never felt less qualified to protect someone, and keep them safe, than I did when Cam asked me if I was there to arrest him.

Fortunately, there was plenty of evidence to show that Dalton and his group of thugs had been harassing Cam before the fight broke out. One of my deputies even confiscated a Snapchat video showing one of Dalton's crew tripping Cam as he tried to walk away when they surrounded him. It was enough to justify a self-defense claim and I knew the county's district attorney wouldn't bring forward charges on assault, knowing they would immediately be tossed out of court. It was going to piss the mayor off even more than he already was, but I was eternally grateful I wasn't going to have to put Cam in cuffs. I was worried about the escalating violence at a bone-deep level and warned the teenager to watch his back. I knew Cam was no stranger to adversity, and I hated that he couldn't seem to catch a break. I hated that I couldn't stand up for him without fearing serious professional and personal repercussions. The only other time I'd felt this helpless was when I watched them lower my mentor in the ground, wondering what more I could have done, feeling that I had somehow failed the man who meant so much to me.

Cam simply shrugged, as if this treatment was to be expected, and thanked me for giving him a heads up about keeping track of everything. I felt his quiet acceptance of the ugliness he faced like an arrow right through my heart. I wanted to hit something. I wanted to knock on the mayor's door and put my fist in his face. I wanted to shake some sense into his son. I felt absolutely filthy that I'd ever been proud to have such a disgusting human being's approval. I was really starting to wonder if this job was worth it. But then again, what if the mayor managed to put someone as easily controllable in the position as Delaney's ex-husband? Kids like Cam wouldn't stand a chance.

It took a minute, but eventually, Wyatt opened the door. He looked as if he'd been sleeping, aside from the glass of amber liquid in his hand. His fair hair was sticking up in random directions. He had a shadow of scruff along his sharp jawline. The only piece of clothing he was wearing was a pair of black boxer briefs. He didn't look particularly happy to see me, but he opened the door and took a step back, wordlessly handing me the glass of whatever he was drinking as I stepped into the darkened interior of his borrowed bunkhouse.

I finished the rest of his drink. It turned out to be an expensive scotch. I could tell by the earthiness, smoothness, and lack of burn as it went down. I stepped carefully as I made my way to the kitchenette to drop the empty glass in the sink. The only light in the room came from the moonlight shining through the windows.

I braced my hands on the edge of the counter and let my head hang heavily. I heard Wyatt moving around in the room behind me, and eventually, a small amount of light filtered through the room as he turned on a lamp.

"No matter how badly you feel, or how frustrated you may be, you need to keep in mind Cam is feeling the same, times one hundred. This was supposed to be a fresh start for that kid. Now, he's facing the same kind of thing that had him running away from home in the first place. He's not facing it on his own this time, which is good, but he's still facing it. You don't get to give up on him. You don't get to pretend this doesn't affect you." There was no mistaking the censure in his voice, and it sliced right through me.

My hands tightened on the edge of the counter and I closed my eyes briefly. "I know all of that." I just had no idea what I was going to do about any of it. But I knew, at the end of the day, I couldn't let anything happen to Cam. Regardless of how it made me look or if it compromised my position as sheriff.

A moment later, I felt warmth press against my back. Wyatt's forehead touched the base of my neck where my head was bent, and his arms wrapped loosely around my waist. I didn't realize how cold I was, that there had been a chill in my blood, until Wyatt's warmth started to seep into me.

"It'll be okay. There are more people interested in doing the right thing than there are people determined to do the wrong thing. We just have to stick together." His palms pressed into my stomach and pulled me closer to his body. We were built pretty similarly, but I still felt like I was surrounded by a bubble of comfort and acceptance with his arms around my midsection.

"I feel guilty." The words felt like they were ripped from the darkest, most hidden portion of my heart. "High school was no picnic for me, but I didn't have to face anything like what Cam is going through. But I should've. If I'd been honest. If I'd been open about who I was, I would've been in the exact same boat as him. I feel like maybe his experience wouldn't be so bad if he wasn't the first to say, 'this is who I am, deal with it.'"

Wyatt made a noise and I felt the brush of his mouth on the base of my neck. The tiny kiss sent chills dancing up and down my spine. "Can't turn back the clock. And even if you could, who knows if being out when you were younger would have made any difference now. You said your family already had issues with you; coming out might've been too much for them. You could've ended up on the streets the way Cam did, and we both know stumbling onto guardian angels like Brynn and Lane is a rarity. Honesty isn't always the best policy. Believe me, I know from first-hand experience."

I remembered that he mentioned things had been even harder for him when his abusive mother found out he was gay.

"Lying doesn't feel like it's the right thing to do anymore. I'm not ashamed of who I am, and it's exhausting always having to pretend." I was tired of it. I just wanted to live my life the same as everyone else. I didn't want to have to give Wyatt a look or silent warning when he touched me in public. I wanted to be free to touch him without worrying about who was watching my every move. I'd finally reached a breaking point I hadn't even been aware I was running toward.

One thing I knew with absolute certainty was that every time things became overwhelming, Wyatt was the person I wanted to turn to. As someone who was used to handling everything on my own, it was a new experience to want to lean on someone else. Especially when that person admitted they might not be staying around forever. I needed to remind myself that Wyatt wasn't permanent, and the support and wise words he offered were temporary. Sooner or later, I was going to be facing heartbreak on top of the existential crisis I was currently going through. I needed to save my strength, because getting through both was going to be a battle.

"You shouldn't be ashamed of who you are. You're working with some pretty good stuff, Sheriff." Wyatt's voice turned husky and his slight East Coast accent was a little more prominent than usual. I grunted in agreement, letting my eyes drift closed when I felt his hands start to work the fabric of my shirt free from my pants. One of his palms hit the lower part of my stomach and my muscles contracted in response. My dick twitched with awareness and started to press insistently against the zipper of my jeans. I think my body did a pretty good job of letting him know he was also working with some pretty good stuff. I liked the way his hands felt on me. There was no hesitation in his caress, no fear. He touched me the way I wanted to touch him from this point forward.

His teeth nipped at the curve of my neck as his quick fingers made fast work of my heavy belt buckle. I tilted my head to the side to give him better access, sighing in satisfaction as the nip turned into a full-on bite. It stung just a little, and I knew I was going to have a mark on that spot tomorrow. One I wasn't going to try to hide.

Wyatt methodically popped open the snaps on my shirt, leaving it fluttered open. He efficiently got my belt unbuckled and my jeans unfastened. I felt like I was caught up in some sort of dreamy haze, as he purposefully pulled me out of my clothes, all while his mouth left a hot trail of bites and kisses up and down the side of my neck. The sensual assault made my knees feel like they were suddenly made of water and forced my heart to thunder loudly inside of my chest. I was always so busy trying to overwhelm him that I was unprepared for what it would be like when he turned my own strategy against me. I wanted to close my eyes and never wake up from this moment because it didn't feel real.

I always had secrets, either from my career, my past, or because of my hidden sexuality, that I constantly lived in fear of being revealed. Wyatt was the first person ever from whom I wasn't hiding anything. He was the first person who I felt knew the real me, and the fact he still let me in tonight, the fact he was still touching me, tasting me, pressing his body against mine as if he couldn't get close enough, was almost too much. I wanted to ask him to stay. I wanted to tell him how important he was, how much this moment meant, but the words got caught behind fear in my throat. I didn't want to pressure him and scare him off. Not now. Not ever.

My jeans ended up around my ankles, caught on my cowboy boots, and the buckle from my belt hit the floor with a loud clang. My own boxer briefs joined them a moment later, as Wyatt worked the stretchy material down my long legs. A second later I was forcibly turned around, his mouth landing squarely against mine, and his toned body beautifully bare as he pressed up against me once again. He put one hand on the counter next to my hip as he leaned into me, and the other he used to rummage around in one of the drawers next to the sink. I heard things clattering around, but didn't get a chance to ask what he was doing because his tongue pushed between my lips and swirled around mine.

I muttered my approval and wrapped a hand around the back of his neck to pull him closer. We both gasped in surprise when the heat of our exposed cocks pressed against each other. The silky-smooth hardness rubbing against my own was enough to make my breath catch and my eyes roll back in my head. He felt so good gliding right up against me. Without thinking about it, I started to reach for both the throbbing and aching shafts. I wanted to hold them against each other. I wanted to rock into him. I wanted to feel him sliding against my hand and along the length of my cock at the same time. I wanted it all, and then I wanted to do it again in as many different locations and positions as I could think of.

Wyatt batted my hand away before I could get a grip on our straining erections. I pulled my mouth free from his punishing kiss to ask what he was thinking, but immediately swallowed the words when I felt his hand encircle both of us. There was something warm and slippery slathered all over his wide palm. When I got my wits back, I made a mental note to ask him why he had lube stashed in the tiny kitchen, or rather, I was going to thank him for being a Boy Scout and always being prepared.

The pressure from Wyatt's hand as it smoothly glided up and down had me breathing hard. The way he played with my mouth while his hand drove me out of my mind had pleasure coiling tightly at the base of my spine and all my extremities tingling in anticipation. Blood rushed from every part of my body to the spot where Wyatt was rubbing our cocks together in a slow, maddening rhythm. It'd been a while since I let anyone handle me this way, and there was no doubt everything Wyatt did was worth the wait.

Since his hands were busy, I used mine to run all over his chiseled torso. I carefully ran my fingertips over the raised scar tissue decorating his shoulder and various other spots on his broad chest. I rolled the pad of my thumb over the erect tip of one of his nipples and felt his body jerk in response. The kiss we were sharing turned a bit more forceful, and I felt the edge of his teeth, letting me know he liked the light caress. I switched to the other side, making him pull his head back so he could growl at me. The sound made my dick even harder, and I swore it pulsed in his hand.

Wyatt tightened his hold as he continued to work us both over. The only sounds in the room were our breathing and the totally erotic sound of flesh on flesh as our cocks rubbed against one another. I swore I could feel the thick vein that ran along the bottom of his shaft throbbing in time to my heartbeat. The sensation was something else, and I wasn't sure how long I was going to last.

I used the hold I had on Wyatt's head to pull him back in for another kiss, needing something to ground me before I exploded in his hand. He whispered my name quietly against my lips and sank into the seductive onslaught of lips and tongue. It was my turn to use my teeth, and when I did, I felt his hips kick against mine and the motion of his hand get erratic. His hand tightened, and I felt his thumb slide over the slippery head of my cock. It was all too much. Too much emotion. Too much pleasure. Too much to lose if everything went wrong down the road.

"I'm right at the edge, Wyatt." I figured I should warn him in case he had other plans than having me explode all over his fingers.

My ass was pressed up against the edge of the counter and the muscles clenched reflexively when Wyatt's thumb circled the flared head of my dick before pressing himself even closer to me. There was hardly any space between either of us, but I wanted to be even closer. I needed to ask Wyatt where this was all going, once I could form words again.

"Good. I like you on the edge, Sheriff."

I growled my response, head thrown back as pleasure spiraled through all my limbs, making my knees weak and my mind go completely blank for a second. I felt my cock jerk in Wyatt's hold and heard him grunt in satisfaction as my completion covered both of us. When I finally managed to peel my eyes open, our gazes locked, and a second later I felt a rush of warmth hit my lower abs and base of my dick.

We were a glorious mess, and I couldn't remember a time in my life when I'd ever felt better.

Wyatt held up his wet, glistening hand and lifted an arrogant eyebrow in my direction. With a smirk, he licked the side of his thumb and told me, "Let's take a shower and go to bed. Things will look different in the morning. No one said we have to solve all the world's problems in one night."

No one said it, but it felt like that was the expectation. Bending to pull off my boots, I asked without looking at him, "What are we doing, pretty boy?"

Did this mean half as much to him as it did to me?

"We don't have to figure that out in one night either." When I finally gathered the courage to look at him, he lifted his non-scarred shoulder and let it drop in a careless shrug. "But this feels like the beginning of something, doesn't it?"

I sighed, and nodded in silent agreement.

The only thing that worried me was if we indeed started something, we either choose to keep it going or waited for it to end. I knew which one of those things I wanted to happen, but had no clue what Wyatt was thinking, and he'd already told me honesty wasn't always the best policy. Would he be truthful if I pressed him about the direction we were headed, or would he tell me what I wanted to hear because it would be so much easier when it came time for him to walk away?

Confused and frustrated, I followed him to the shower, knowing I was going to need answers one way or the other... even if the truth did ultimately hurt.

CHAPTER 14

WYATT

ARE YOU READY FOR this?"

Rodie's voice was a raspy growl next to my ear. I was pressed up against the slippery tiles of the walk-in shower. My forehead was resting against the slick surface. I kept my eyes closed as one of Rodie's hands skimmed over my bare chest, while the fingers of the other unerringly moved in and out of my clenching hole. Sure, the shower started out as a way for both of us to get clean before crashing out for the night. I wasn't surprised things quickly turned dirty underneath the pouring water and heated up in the swirling steam. His hands were everywhere, scrambling common sense and making my skin feel like it was buzzing with electricity.

If I was being truthful, I would admit that I knew exactly where things were headed when I made the decision to let him in this evening. And maybe I'd been awake, waiting for him to arrive, because I knew that he would. I knew exactly what was in store, so I'd been ready for this long before he put his hands on me, and I'd worked to prepare my body for the obvious next step. Though I appreciated his consideration and the time he was investing to make sure I was as turned on and eager as he was.

Outwardly, Rodie didn't come across as a thoughtful and tender man. He was all rough edges because of his childhood and time in the military. It did something to my insides to know he took deliberate care when it came to pleasing his partner, and that he put effort into letting me know I mattered to him, that the intimacy and attraction we shared was special and worth more than a quick fuck in the dark.

Rodie and I may clash in a lot of ways, but when all the barriers dropped and we were stripped bare, both literally and figuratively, we were more than compatible. I had a normal sex drive, and an active libido, but I had never met someone I couldn't keep my hands off until the good sheriff came into my life. It didn't matter if we disagreed in the daylight. Here, in the dim light of the moon, we were on exactly the same page and had the same objective... to make each other feel good and make the other forget whomever had come before.

With my body clenching and tightening with his every stroke, and my insides feeling like they were lit up and glowing as flames of desire flickered throughout my body, there was no comparison to any man who had been in my life before Rodie. No one else left their touch burned into my skin, nor their kiss branded on my mouth the way he did. He seemed so much bigger and brighter than any of the shadows that had passed through in a blur. He felt so solid, so real, and I was secretly a little afraid of how powerful the emotions he brought to the surface were.

I didn't know if I was coming or going, and he didn't know how to be the man he was meant to be. There were so many unanswered questions between us, but none of it seemed to matter when Rodie pressed closer, his chest practically glued to my back because of his wet skin and how tightly he was holding me. I felt the heat of his erection as it rubbed against the curve of my ass. Since I wasn't sure how stable I would be if I moved, I'd made him leave the warmth of the shower to retrieve the lube left in the kitchen, as well as a condom from the stash I had in the same drawer.

He was right when he joked I was always prepared, but the truth was, I'd made a stop at a drug store after one of my sessions with Miranda, because there was no denying the direction things were headed with Rodie after that first life-altering kiss. It was a kiss that would inevitably lead to other things, and I wanted to make sure I was prepared for whatever Rodie threw my way.

I still couldn't bend and move the way I used to, so once again we'd had to get creative. Standing upright kept pressure off my bad shoulder but made my injured knee shaky. Fortunately, Rodie was strong enough, I could lean against him, and he managed to keep us both upright. Who knew sex was going to be my biggest motivating factor in getting my free range of motion back?

"I want you, want this." My voice was strained and low. A soft chuckle escaped, but it turned into a moan of pure pleasure when Rodie's questing fingers found that spot inside that was bound to make a man lose his mind. "Don't let me fall."

There was definitely a double meaning behind those words. It might be a bit too late to stop myself from falling for him, but that was easier to accept than the image of me ending up at his feet in a naked heap because my leg gave out.

I felt him grin against my shoulder where his mouth was resting in between kisses. "If you fall, I'll catch you."

I wanted to tell him the same thing, I would catch him if he fell. However, I was the one backing him closer and closer to the edge of a cliff where he'd never been comfortable. I didn't want him to hide anymore. I wanted him to be a voice and an inspiration for kids like Cam. I wanted him to have the chance to be comfortable in his own skin. The truth was, I was tripping him up and making him fall, and I didn't feel bad about it. I did feel pretty terrible not knowing if I would be around when it was time to pick him up. Sooner rather than later, I needed to figure out my life. I needed to put my finger on what really was going to make me happy, aside from all the glorious things Rodie was making me feel.

I was happy right now, and about to get even happier, because Rodie replaced his flexing fingers with the tip of his cock. I sucked in a breath and felt my hands curl into fists at the initial burn and stretch of his invasion. Rodie did a good job preparing my body for his entrance, but it'd still been more than a minute since I'd been with anyone, and he was working with equipment that was impressive in a lot of ways. I was going to feel him well into tomorrow, but I loved every minute of my body slowly quivering and quaking as I adjusted to having him inside. I liked to give and to receive, but typically the men I dated just assumed I wanted to be the one on top. I always blamed the badge and gun, as well as my uptight personality, for the assumption. It was kind of thrilling Rodie didn't ask what I wanted or what I liked. He just seemed to instinctively know.

I also understood he was pretty open-minded when it came to positions and preferences. He hadn't batted an eye when I fingered him awake the first time he crashed with me.

I heard his breath catch and felt his teeth dig into the curve of my shoulder. The fingers of his hand, which was resting protectively over my heart, curled against my skin, his short nails leaving marks. We were both going to look a little worse for the wear in the morning, but these tell-tale signs of love, sex, and everything in-between were beautiful. They were reminders of a beautiful act between people who cared about one another, not memories of pain and suffering like all the scars were. Any spot left on my skin from Rodie's mouth and hands I would wear proudly. I silently hoped he felt the same. I didn't want him to look in the mirror and feel shame when he saw where I'd been all over his skin. I wanted him to be pleased, the same way I was. I wanted him to remember me, because I knew it was going to be impossible for me to ever forget him.

I wrapped my damp hand around my cock when Rodie took another step closer. There was zero space between my back and his front. I let out a long breath once he was fully seated inside of me, my entire body tightening in response to feeling so full and stretched. Rodie's teeth locked onto my shoulder as he started to thrust with a forceful and purposeful rhythm. He braced his free hand on my hip, fingers digging into my flesh, to hold me up and hold me still as his hips retreated and collided against my backside.

The sound of wet skin on wet skin, the sounds of harsh breathing and low grunts of satisfaction, rang between my ears. It was enough to have my dick kicking in excitement within my grasp. I felt my balls tingle and pull tight between my legs, desire surging thick and syrupy in my veins. I gave the shaft in my hand a squeeze to still some of the churning desire. I wanted to prolong the moment, wanted to draw every second of pleasure as long as I could.

Rodie muttered my name as his rhythm picked up speed and lost some of its finesse. I closed my eyes and let my head drop, the tile cool against my skin. His hold on my hip tightened until it was almost painful, and I swore I could feel every pulse and throb of his cock where it was pressed inside of me. The tapered head tapped against that hot spot, and I knew I would've hit the ground if he hadn't been holding me. The onslaught of sensation was almost too much.

Wetness from the tip of my cock made my hand slippery as it continued to glide up and down my rigid shaft. I bit back a moan when I felt Rodie's hand wrap around, so we were both working me over as he continued to thrust inside my body. His breath was warm on the side of my neck, and the quiet swear words slipping out of his lips caused me to grin. I enjoyed his loss of composure and how he seemed to be just slightly wild and out of control. He was so bossy normally; it was flattering to know he wanted me so much he forgot his insistent need to be in charge. He still let an order slip here and there, but he was so focused on driving us both to the pinnacle of pleasure, he couldn't string a coherent command together.

"So good. So tight and warm. I'm not going to last much longer." I grinned at the quiet admission, moving my hand faster as he relentlessly worked my prostate.

"Let go." The words were rough, because I was as close to coming as he was. I couldn't tell him I would catch him, but I wouldn't let him fall alone.

His hips ground against my ass, and I felt his cock jerk and spasm inside of me. He panted his completion along the side of my neck, and I felt his teeth tug on my ear. He whispered my name, and the soft, reverent sound was what ultimately pushed my own release. My dick painted the tiles in front of me as I sighed heavily in satisfaction. My body was fully satiated, and my mind felt like it was full of cotton candy. I might not be totally healthy at the moment, but if he asked if I was happy, I'd have to tell him I was. I would be hard pressed to pick another time in my life when I felt this good.

We both groaned when Rodie pulled back, separating our bodies with a slick sound. He squeezed my hip, fingers dragging over the red marks he'd left there. I felt his lips brush against the back of my neck. He asked if I was okay to stand on my own, and when I gave him a sleepy nod, he moved away to take care of the condom and grab us a couple of towels to dry off.

I let him guide me toward the bed in the center of the room, feeling like I was walking through a dream. I was almost asleep when he laid down next to me and tossed the comforter over us. I was too spent and too tired to protest when he yanked me against his broad chest. I was also too far gone to worry when he whispered, "We have to talk about this eventually."

Maybe this meant the seriously awesome sex, but I had a gut feeling it meant something else. He was going to want answers about what all of this meant between us, and I wasn't sure I had one he wanted to hear. I feigned sleep so I wouldn't have to respond, real sleep hovering on the periphery. He must've been willing to let the subject drop, because the next thing I knew, the morning sun was bleeding into the small space.

I woke with a yawn, stretching my arms above my head as I became slowly aware of the hard body beneath mine. I turned my head to look at a sleeping Rodie Collins. He really was beautiful in a dark and brooding kind of way. He didn't look peaceful while he slept. He still had a furrow between his eyebrows and a slant to his mouth. It almost looked like all the things haunting him while he was awake got worse when he was resting. It had to be exhausting constantly holding a mask in place and praying it didn't slip.

A moment later, an alarm screamed loud and shrill from his phone, pulling those brilliant green eyes open. He rubbed a hand over his face, pausing to scratch the dark stubble that covered his chin.

"I gotta go to work." He stretched similar to the way I did, rolling to the side of the bed and climbing out, so he could find his discarded jeans. "But we do need to talk, Wyatt."

I rolled my stiff shoulders, muttering, "You might not like what I have to say, Sheriff." I wasn't going to make a promise I wasn't sure I could keep.

Rodie sighed and turned to look at me, he was gearing up to say something, probably to start a fight, when there was a knock at the door.

I bolted upright, holding the sheet around my waist as I scrambled to get to my feet. It was probably just Cam with breakfast from the main house like it was every morning, but in case it was one of the Warners or my brother, the last thing I wanted was for Rodie to answer the door half-dressed.

Only I wasn't fast enough and almost ended up on the floor with the sheet twisted around me. Rodie clearly wasn't afraid of anything or anyone at the moment, because he put his shirt on and went to the door without buttoning it. Anyone on the other side would know exactly what we were up to, and then I was going to have to explain myself to more than just him.

"Oh, hey, Sheriff." I heard Cam's voice try to cover his surprise. "I brought Wyatt breakfast from Brynn. I don't think she knew you were here or she would've packed more." He was such a freaking good kid. The Warners were lucky to have him, and so was this town he now called home.

Rodie chuckled. "No worries. I'm on my way out. Give Wyatt a minute to get up and going. He had a late night and he's moving slowly this morning."

I got to my feet as Rodie stepped onto the front porch, pulling the door shut behind him, and doing up the buttons on his uniform shirt as he went.

Outside, I heard Cam ask, "What's wrong?" as I flew around the room, trying to pick up hastily removed clothing and any other signs of the debauchery I'd indulged in last night. I tugged on a pair of track pants and a t-shirt, ran a comb through my hair, and brushed my teeth so I could at least pretend to be a respectable grown-up.

Rodie's deep voice rumbled that he felt like someone was watching them. Then he told Cam to have a good day and to stay out of trouble until his suspension from school was over. Cam agreed, telling Rodie it was probably just one of the family keeping an eye on him from the big house. He mumbled that everyone was really worried lately, and I heard Rodie apologize to the teenager for not being able to do more. He really was a good guy, and I felt bad that I was now the hard place pushing him against the unyielding rock of expectations.

When I heard his SUV start up, I went to the door and pulled it open, ushering Cam inside. I stuck my head outside to watch Rodie drive away, and I also got a weird prickle on the back of my neck. My instincts had kept me alive in more than one dangerous situation, and I agreed with Rodie that something was off, even if nothing on the massive, sprawling property immediately looked amiss.

"You're banging the sheriff." It wasn't a question, and Cam looked surprisingly pleased as he made the bold statement.

I sighed and took the breakfast basket from him. "I don't know what I'm doing." Which was the story of my life. "I didn't find out he was interested in me until a couple of days ago. No one in town really knows he's gay, so it's complicated. Better to keep it quiet."

Cam took a seat at the table, dark eyebrows lifting. "He's very good looking. You guys look great together. I didn't know he was gay either, but I'm not surprised. He's been very encouraging with me, and pretty supportive. It felt like more than just his job."

I groaned and dragged my hands over my face. "Don't give me your seal of approval, kid. I'm already having a hard time trying to remain objective and level-headed where he's concerned."

Cam chuckled and reached for the goodie basket so he could paw through it. "You're both these larger-than-life kind of men. It's like if Bucky and Captain America hooked up." He wiggled his eyebrows at me and flashed a smirk. "That's super-hot when you think about it."

I groaned again and threw my arm over my eyes. It was hot, but I wasn't anyone's hero anymore, and I didn't want to think about Rodie being as broken as Bucky.

CHAPTER 15

RODIE

"YOU NEED A TETANUS shot, Sheriff."

I bit back a dirty word as the doctor poked at the wound on my hand. I got tangled up with some rusty barbed wire helping one of the local ranchers wrangle an unruly steer back into its pen. There were always unexpected parts of the job when you were a law enforcement officer in a rural town. Luckily, the laceration on my hand and wrist was the worst I'd been injured since taking the job.

I waited impatiently for the medical staff in the ER to finish wrapping my hand and suffered through the shot, since it'd been years since my last one. Working with a busted hand for the next few days was going to be a challenge. Things had been busy at the sheriff's station over the last week. It seemed like as soon as the mayor and Byron announced I was no longer running unopposed, the town was doing its best to put me to the test. I was dealing with the kind of crime we didn't typically see in Sheridan, and I was working the kind of hours that were bound to wear a man down and make him careless... hence my lacerated hand. It rubbed me the wrong way that everywhere I turned, someone was in my face asking how I felt about the upcoming election. They wanted to know if I was worried. They asked if I thought Byron was a worthy opponent. I couldn't get a moment of peace, and there'd been no time to pin Wyatt down so we could have a heart to heart, or another round of mind-blowing sex, either of which I'd take after the past few days.

I hadn't seen the man in days, and the uncertainty and repressed desire put me in a foul mood. My deputies were tip-toeing around me, and I couldn't blame them for handling me with caution.

Holding my injured hand and flexing my fingers to see how much I could move them in the bandage, I sucked in a breath as pain shot up my arm. I was lucky I escaped without a bunch of stitches, but it still hurt like a bitch.

I was driving toward the station when I caught sight of a familiar figure running across Main Street toward the diner in the center of town. I pulled the SUV into a parking spot in front of the restaurant and followed Cam into the building. The teen was hovering uncertainly at the hostess stand, eyes wide as he took in the old-fashioned interior of the diner. It occurred to me that Cam had been in Sheridan for several months now, but he usually stuck close to the Warner Ranch and didn't venture out much. I clapped a hand on his shoulder, making him jump and spin around in surprise. With his crazy dyed hair, huge dark eyes, and ultra-trendy clothes, he looked a little bit like an anime character come to life. He definitely didn't look like the other regulars visiting the diner.

"What's up, kid?" I gave him what I hoped was a reassuring grin and motioned a waitress over to show him to a seat. I followed him to a booth, watching as he nervously played with the menu in front of him.

"I was going stir-crazy at the ranch. I asked Wyatt if I could tag along when he came to town for his physical therapy appointment for a change of scenery." He made a face. "I never thought I would miss going to school. I was so behind when I first started since I had to drop out when my parents kicked me out. But I caught up pretty quick. I hope this suspension doesn't screw everything up for me."

I asked for a cup of coffee when the waitress stopped by. I had to repeat myself because she was staring at Cam like he was some kind of alien lifeform. He asked for pancakes and handed the menu over. The waitress walked away muttering something under her breath, but Cam seemed immune to the reaction.

"Is someone bringing you the school work you're missing while you're on suspension?" I was sure neither Brynn nor Lane would let him fall behind.

Cam nodded, playing with the straw on the table in front of him. "Yeah. A couple of the girls have kept me up to date. I guess I need to accept they might actually want to be my friend and aren't just hanging around me out of curiosity. A few of my teachers won't accept any work while I'm suspended, so my grades are going to suffer in those subjects no matter what I do." He shrugged as if it was no big deal, but I could tell he was bothered by the situation.

"I'll double-check if Dalton has the same teachers. He should face the same consequences." I wouldn't put it past some at the school to favor the other boy, and not just because he was the mayor's son.

Cam shrugged again, finally lifting his gaze to meet mine. "I don't care about that. I just have to worry about myself."

Of course, he felt that way. He'd spent his entire young life looking out for himself, especially when the people who were supposed to love and protect him turned their backs. Unfortunately, I knew that feeling all too well. There was still time for people, for me, to prove to Cam the world wasn't against him, and it was a better place because of kids like him.

I sighed and reached for the sugar when my coffee was set down in front of me. "I'll worry about it. Things should be fair for all students going to that school."

Cam flashed a sad smile and thanked the waitress when she dropped off his plate of food. She looked a little startled at his perfect manners and finally smiled back at him. Once folks got past their initial reaction to how he looked, they quickly realized he was a good kid with more wisdom than most of the adults I dealt with on a daily basis.

Cam changed the subject, grinning at me as he dug into his breakfast. "So, you and Wyatt, huh? Didn't see that coming."

My spine stiffened and I couldn't keep my eyes from darting nervously around to see who may have overheard him. I was annoyed by my own reaction, and hated that Cam obviously took note of the uncomfortable response. I still couldn't shake the feeling that someone was watching me. I'd had a tingle on the back of my neck since the morning at Wyatt's bunkhouse. I was probably being paranoid with the election looming and the mayor in my face every time I turned around. But the impending sense of doom wouldn't leave me and it was making me hyper-vigilant.

I cleared my throat and picked up my coffee. "Wyatt's a good guy. I'm glad his brother convinced him to come to Sheridan for a little while. I've been interested in getting to know him better for some time now."

Cam's eyebrows lifted and his dark gaze sharpened. "Wyatt's more than a good guy. He's an actual hero. He's survived things that would destroy another man. He puts everything on the line for those he cares about when no one did the same for him. He deserves better than someone just interested in *getting to know him better*."

Ouch.

Taken to task by a teenager. And he wasn't wrong. Wyatt did deserve better than deflection and denial.

"It's complicated." It was a lame excuse, but it was all I had at the moment.

Cam snorted. "Yeah, I know all about complicated. But if you can't find a way to make it uncomplicated, you're going to lose your shot at having something great."

"I'll keep that in mind, kid."

He nodded his approval and tucked into his food. We kept the conversation light as he finished up, and I offered to walk him back to Miranda's office to meet up with Wyatt. Sure, I had ulterior motives. I wanted to see Wyatt. I could admit I'd missed him this week, maybe not out loud where someone might overhear, but in my heart, there was no denying the longing. The empty echo in my chest was annoyingly loud when it was just me alone with my thoughts and regrets.

The tingle on the back of my neck intensified as we walked out of the diner. I couldn't shake the feeling of prying eyes all over me. I whipped my head around, scanning the street up and down, but didn't see anything out of place.

Cam tilted his head, indicating he was going to run back across the street. I was a second away from telling him not to jay-walk when my name was suddenly called from the window of a BMW. I knew it was Delaney without seeing her. I knew there was no escaping her once she had me in her sights. I waved off Cam, telling him to be safe and watch for cars if he was going to run across the street. He rolled his eyes at me and reached out a hand to knock his fist against my shoulder in a familiar manner. He quietly stated Wyatt was going to be jealous over our breakfast date before jogging away while laughing lightly.

I kept an eye on him until he was safely on the other side of the road. I knew Delaney was going to be heated that I made her wait, and I wasn't wrong. She was practically seething by the time I made my way over to the car.

I put my injured hand on the roof of the car and bent down to look inside. Delaney had her hands curled around the steering wheel and was watching the spot where Cam had disappeared.

"Get in the car, Rodie."

I was surprised she used my name instead of calling me Sheriff.

"I've got to get back to the station. It's been crazy this week. I have paperwork piling up and a new call every few minutes." I was busy, and the last place I wanted to be was alone with her anywhere.

Delaney turned her head. Her face was set in a tense expression and I could practically feel the way her eyes tried to burn holes into me.

"Get in the car now, Sheriff. Let's just say that you'll be sorry if you don't." Everything about her demeanor screamed of a threat, and I didn't like that feeling one damn bit.

"Something tells me I'll be even more sorry if I do get in the car. Just tell me what you want, Delaney." I still had a full day of work to tackle and wasn't in any mood for her distractions and games.

"Pick up the envelope on the seat." She pointed a manicured finger at the manila envelope.

Sighing in frustration, I reached for it. "What is this?"

"Look for yourself." She bit out each word while continuing to glare daggers in my direction.

I went still as stone when I pulled the first picture out of the envelope.

The image showed me buttoning up my shirt while standing on the porch of Wyatt's bunkhouse. Cam was standing next to me, his head tossed back as he laughed at something I said. Out of context, it looked like an intimate moment caught between me and the teenager.

"What in the hell is this?" There were several pictures from the same morning in the envelope, and when I looked over at Delaney, she had her cell phone in her hand. On the screen was a picture of me and Cam walking out of the diner. She swiped angrily, showing another image of the teenager playfully tapping on my shoulder.

"Do you think I'm stupid, Rodie?" She sounded so furious, it was almost hard to understand her.

"No. I think you're dangerous." I knew there was nothing behind the pictures, but they looked damning to the untrained and suspicious eye.

"You've turned me down and insulted me time and time again. I knew there had to be a reason why. I'm going to end you, Rodie Collins. And I'm going to ruin that kid's life." She sounded totally unhinged and when she finally looked at me, I could see all kinds of crazy in her eyes. "How dare you make a fool of me and bring that kind of disgusting behavior into this town."

"Did you hire someone to follow me?" I couldn't keep the shock and exasperation out of my voice. I knew something hadn't been quite right the last few days, but couldn't put my finger on it. I should've been more aware of my surroundings and more vigilant when I felt like I was being followed. I was going to have to ask the Warners if they had some kind of surveillance out at the ranch. If they didn't, they needed to get some after this.

Delaney's jaw clenched and her knuckles turned white where she gripped the steering wheel. "I did what I had to do since you weren't honest, or forthcoming, with answers."

I swore and banged my hurt hand on the hood of the luxury car. "I was honest. I told you I wasn't interested. That's the only explanation you need. This is crazy. Something isn't right with you." I shook my head. "It's one thing to come after me, but to threaten an innocent kid because you couldn't get your way..." I shook my head at her in disgust. "That's a special kind of fucked up."

She turned in her seat, pointing a blood red nail at my face. "You're the one who's fucked up! How dare you corrupt a child like that."

I barked out a low laugh and threw the offending photos back into her car. "Your boss is the only one out to corrupt that child. He's a good kid who has had nothing but bad luck. I'm keeping an eye on him because I know his history and how hard a time he's had since school started. Those pictures don't tell half the story." I arched an eyebrow up and smirked at her. "I wasn't at the ranch to see Cam, I was there to see Wyatt Bryant. I spent the night with him and just happened to run into Cam in the morning on my way out." It was absolute honesty, maybe the most truth I'd ever spoken in my adult life, and it felt good to let it out. Damn good. But I wasn't about to let her, or anyone else, drag Cam into the middle of a scandal just so they could defeat me.

"No one is going to believe that when I make these pictures public. You're barely holding onto your position as it is. What do you think folks will think when they find out you're a homosexual and prey on young boys in the area?"

"Jesus Christ." I banged my forehead on the frame of the door and let out a string of swear words. This was beyond not playing fair, and while I was annoyed at being backed into a corner, I was more worried about what this kind of gossip would mean for Cam. Everything inside of me was screaming that I had to protect the poor kid. "What's the point of all this, Delaney? What do you want from me?"

"You know what I want, Sheriff." She narrowed her eyes and let her gaze drag pointedly across my face.

"You've got to be shitting me." I smacked my bandaged hand on the roof of the car once again. "You just heard me tell you I'm interested in men, that I have no desire to be with a woman, regardless of who she is, and you still want to blackmail me into being with you? Your wiring is all screwy, Delaney."

"Figure it out, Rodie. Give me what I want, or I'll make sure you not only lose the election, but every single ounce of respect you have in this town. Both you and that boy will have to leave Sheridan by the time I'm done with you." She tapped the picture with a finger and turned her head so that she was once again looking out the windshield. "You have through the weekend to decide what you're going to do."

With that parting threat, she rolled up the window and left me standing there, staring after her in shock. I put my hands on my hips and breathed in the dust her tires kicked up. I felt a little like I'd been kicked in the gut. Not only had I come out to someone I didn't like, didn't trust, and wanted nothing to do with, I now also had to decide the best way to deal with the situation and confession so Cam wasn't caught in the cross-fire.

I knew for certain I wasn't going to give in to her demands.

There was no way in hell I was ever going to sleep with Delaney Hall, no matter how dirty she played. I wasn't about to be her puppet, because then I would always be hanging at the end of her strings.

Kicking at the ground, I swore again, marshaling my spinning thoughts together. I looked across the street at Miranda's office, knowing the first thing I had to do was warn Wyatt and prepare Cam for the impending shit-show.

We needed a plan. One that was foolproof.

I needed help. I needed someone to talk to, someone who would tell me everything would be okay. Since my CO died, I hadn't had someone to lean on when life got overwhelming. But now there was Wyatt. He might not be there down the road, but he was here now, and I desperately needed his shoulder to lean on.

CHAPTER 16

WYATT

"**Y**OU REALLY DON'T HAVE to worry about me." Cam's voice was surprisingly calm, and he appeared to be more worried about Rodie than himself.

To be fair, Rodie seemed to be one second away from losing any and all control he had over himself. His eyes were wide and wild. His normally swarthy complexion was alarmingly pale. He couldn't seem to focus on anything, and just kept repeating a litany of swear words. He was stressed in a way I hadn't seen before, but most of his concern was centered on how Delaney and the mayor were going to spin their supposed evidence in order to hurt Cam. He didn't seem to be fazed at all that the secret he'd been so desperate to keep hidden for so long was about to be on the tips of everyone's tongues.

"This isn't good." Miranda was also worried. She'd been frowning even more than usual ever since Rodie burst into her office exclaiming there was an emergency and he needed all hands on deck to minimize the damage.

The older woman held up her cell phone and gave it a little shake. "I just got an email stating there's going to be an emergency town hall meeting on Monday afternoon. The mayor sent out the notice, and I have no doubts it's tied to all of this.

He's going to make as big of a spectacle as he can out of outing Rodie and dragging Cam through the mud, virtually taking care of two problems in one fell swoop. I'm so mad at myself for ever voting for that scumbag."

I reached for the phone with my free hand. My other was threaded through Rodie's soft, dark hair. He had his head pressed against my stomach and his arms wrapped loosely around my waist. Every so often, I would feel a tremor run through his tense muscles, and I could see how stiff and rigid the rest of his body was. The man used to run black ops missions without breaking a sweat, and here he was turned inside out because he was terrified for a sixteen-year-old boy.

I cupped the back of Rodie's head and muttered over and over that we'd figure something out and he didn't have to worry. He might worry about making enemies and rubbing the locals the wrong way, but I had no such qualms. I would ruffle every feather I found, and I had zero fear of going up against the mayor and Delaney. The only people who mattered in this entire equation were already on my side and were, more importantly, in the right. I didn't give a single fuck if everyone else ended up as collateral damage when I was done taking down the mayor and his minions.

"Wait a minute. Didn't Delaney tell you that you had through the weekend to decide what you wanted to do? Why announce the town hall meeting before knowing your decision?" Miranda shook her head in confusion.

Before I could answer, Cam jumped in. Always wise beyond his years, the kid knew exactly what the mayor was planning. "Because, even if the sheriff suddenly decided to give in to her demands, the mayor is still determined to get me out of that school and away from his son. Rodie might be in the clear if he bows to the assistant's wishes, but they never intended to let me be." He sighed heavily and shoved an irritated hand through his bright hair. "No one has wanted to get rid of me this badly since my dad threw me out of the house and told me I was no longer his son."

Still caressing the back of Rodie's head, I shot out an arm and locked it around Cam's neck, pulling him in for a tight hug. We all ended up in a shaking hug, the emotions zipping around us, painful and sharp enough to hurt anyone who got close enough to touch.

"It's okay if people like your dad and this idiot mayor don't want you, Cam, because that type never appreciates what they've got. You would never be good enough for people like that, no matter how hard you tried. But Lane and Brynn, the rest of the Warners, Rodie and I can see how amazing you are without even trying. We don't just want you; we need you. You complete this family, kiddo, and none of us would trade you for the world. If you think it's a hardship on any one of us to take down a small-minded bigot on your behalf, you're mistaken. It's an honor to fight this fight for you... with you. You are an inspiration, Cam. Your life can be whatever you want it to be, and I'm damn sure going to keep the path clear for you on your way to figuring it out."

It was a bold declaration. One that made it sound like I was sticking around longer than I planned. The longer I was in Sheridan surrounded by people who meant so much to me, in so many different ways, I was realizing that that elusive feeling of family I'd always been chasing after might've fallen into my lap. Rodie lifted his head at my admission, and the anguish in his green eyes hit me hard. He was a man who was always composed and carried himself with an admirable amount of confidence. None of that was anywhere to be seen at the moment. Instead, he looked like the scared teenager who didn't have anywhere to turn when the world was against him. I couldn't imagine how challenging his childhood had been growing up here, or what he was going through right now, but I did know I was done playing nice. I might not be capable of taking down an entire drug cartel single-handedly like I used to, but I knew deep in my gut the close-minded mayor was no match for me in the great scheme of things.

"I'll take care of this. For both of you." It was a promise I knew I would have no problem keeping. A spark of something that felt a lot like how I used to feel when I had to protect Webb started to burn in the center of my heart.

Cam grinned at me and pulled away from the awkwardly intense hug. He bopped the top of my shoulder with his hand and told me, "Have I ever told you I wanna be you when I grow up? Seriously, you are the best role model I could've ever asked for, Wyatt. I don't know if you know it, but you've made such a huge difference in my life." He shrugged slightly and looked down at his sneakers in embarrassment. "If you weren't around, I can't guarantee I wouldn't have been so frustrated with the situation that I bolted. I love Lane and Brynn. I will never be able to put words to how much I adore them and appreciate all they've done for me, but sometimes it's nice to have someone around who's been there. Who's walked in the same shoes." I wasn't always proud of my past or so sure about the road I'd traveled to get where I was now. So, it was nice to hear that I'd managed to pull together a life that was enviable to a kid who had seen and done it all. A little voice in the back of my head demanded I be a man who continued to make choices Cam could look up to in the future.

I could see the distress in Rodie's gaze as I stepped out from between his legs. He was sitting on one of Miranda's rolling stools, shoulders slumped forward, and the frown on his face was so fierce that he looked scary. I put my palm on the top of his head and lowered my head so our noses were practically touching. I heard his breath catch.

"You do what you gotta do to protect yourself, Rodie. Don't let that dirty politician win. I won't let anything happen to Cam. Two days isn't a lot to work with, but it's enough. I will find something on the mayor and that assistant of his. No way do they play this down and dirty without having a closet full of skeletons hidden somewhere." I was going to drag every single secret and scandal I could find out into the light.

Rodie sighed and dragged a hand down his face. He suddenly looked every single one of his forty-some years and exhausted beyond measure.

"I've never stooped down to their level. Not when I was younger. Not when I came back and they all treated me like a stranger. I don't want to become like the people I despise just to protect my job... and my reputation." He sounded sad and defeated, which made my blood boil. No one should have to resort to conniving and underhanded tactics in order to justify their mere existence. It wasn't right, but I couldn't sit back and watch this scenario unfold without doing something to protect the people I cared about. "Maybe it's better if I just quit. The easiest thing might be to walk away."

Rodie's statement made my back teeth grind together.

When I was a teenager and met my very first boyfriend, I thought I'd finally found something and someone who was mine. It was the first time I let myself relax and act like a normal teenager. I got swept away in all the new emotions I was experiencing and let myself be lured into the idea I was no longer facing the cold, cruel world on my own. Only my mother popped up out of nowhere, as she was prone to do, and caught me and the other boy in the middle of an intimate moment. She lost her mind, called us both names, threatened to kick me out of the apartment I paid for, and tell the other boy's parents what we were up to when unsupervised. I arrogantly believed the boy thought I was special, that he cared as much about me as I did about him. I thought I'd finally found someone to fight for me.

But all that was too much to ask of a teenager who'd always had things pretty easy in his life.

He was afraid of my mother and the truth. He was scared to rock the boat and understood how easily replaceable young love was. He had a new boyfriend the next week, and I was left holding the burden of yet another betrayal. It'd been easy for him to quit, to walk away. For me, that was never the case, and I couldn't stomach the thought of Rodie throwing in the towel without even trying to fight for what was right. Without even trying to fight for me.

I put a hand out and grasped Rodie's chin. I tilted his head back, forcing his troubled gaze to meet mine. I was ready to jump into a lecture about the message he'd send if he walked away. To Cam. To the people of Sheridan. To the mayor and Delaney. And maybe most importantly, to me. My crush on the stoic sheriff had taken on a life of its own and grown into something bigger, scarier. There were real feelings under the desire and chemistry we shared. I was genuinely worried about the man and what would happen if he backed down at this stage in his life. If he let someone get away with pulling his strings because he was so determined to keep hiding, then what kind of life and relationship could we possibly have going forward? It took everything I had to pull myself out of the shadows, and I wasn't about to go back to dancing in the dark just because Rodie was the first man I could really see myself having a future with.

Before I could launch into the million reasons why walking away was a bad idea, Rodie wrapped his fingers around my wrist and pulled my hand away from his face. Turning my hand over in his, I froze when I felt the press of his lips against the center of my palm. It was a soft, sweet little kiss. One that could easily be overlooked, but for some reason felt incredibly important. The tiny gesture in front of an audience was more than I imagined I'd ever get from him, but it signified a huge step, not only for our relationship, but for him, as well. He wasn't going to hide forever. He was going to step out of the shadows in his own way.

"I'm not going to let anyone run me out of town again. I left to escape the judgment and gossip I knew would suffocate me when I was younger. I know now, you can't ever outrun your problems. They just follow you to wherever you're hiding unless you face them head-on. I wanted to avoid the judgment and gossip as an adult because I didn't want it to affect my job. But I realize my choices make it seem like I'm ashamed of who I am and who I love. I'm not. And it's about time I start acting that way. I'm not going to lose anything to the mayor or Delaney. I'm not giving them the power to control me."

He moved to his feet so suddenly that the rolling chair shot across the room from the momentum. The wheels screeched across the tile as Rodie stood in front of me, everything and everyone in the room melting away. He put his rough, skilled hands on each of my cheeks and looked directly into my eyes. His sincerity and fear were palpable. But so was his determination to hold onto something bigger than being a small-town sheriff, and even more important than proving the people were wrong.

"I won't be happy, really, truly happy, until I get to live my life to the fullest. No more accepting the bare minimum and calling it good enough. I would never let Cam get stuck in a situation like this, where he's hiding and lying to fit in, and I know I won't be able to keep you if I keep lying to myself and everyone else. I don't know how long I have you, but I want the minutes we are fortunate to share to be open and honest. I don't want you to doubt me and the feelings I have for you. I need you to know I'm willing to give it all up for you, but not before I fight for what's right."

I grabbed his face again, pulling him closer so I could feel his heart pounding. "I don't want you to give up anything you've worked for. I want you to face the fear you've been carrying around for so long. Maybe it's so big inside of you because you've never let it out into the light. Doubt and insecurity grow and thrive in the dark, but when you pull them into the light, they often aren't as scary as you think."

He nodded solemnly, head lowering until our lips were a breath apart. Immediately my body lit up and leaned instinctively toward the heat he generated. My dick got hard, and my mind went in a hundred different, dirty directions. It was a serious and troubling conversation. I wanted to help Rodie out. I wanted to give him sage advice and promise things would work themselves out in the end. But I also wanted to push him down on the ground, crawl up on top of him, and distract him with every trick I'd learned. I wanted to make all of him feel better. His body. His mind. His soul. I wanted him to find peace within himself and realize who he was. He was a man worthy of being looked up to, and one who had done more than enough to earn the respect of the town that formerly shunned him. It was on the tip of my tongue to tell him that he didn't need those small-minded idiots when he had me and everyone else in his corner.

He lowered his head, our lips no longer pretending to touch, but locked together in a kiss that sent my head spinning and had my hands grasping frantically at the front of his shirt. Distantly I heard Cam let out a loud wolf whistle and Miranda offer up a round of applause, but I was too focused on the sensations Rodie sent spiraling through my body. One little touch and I was ready to lose my mind. Ready to go to war for this man. Ready to promise him I would stay to fight by his side.

When I pulled back to take a much-needed breath, I was charmed by the red splotches on Rodie's cheeks. He looked so cute all flustered and unsure. I reached up and grasped the back of his head, pulling him forward so our foreheads touched.

"Whatever your next step is, know you aren't taking it alone. I'm here, and I will follow you to hell and back." It was as close as I could get to saying I would stay for him.

He kissed the end of my nose which made Cam laugh and Miranda release a dreamy sigh. "Don't follow me. Walk by my side, and let's take them all on as a united front." Rodie squeezed my hand and let it fall. "It's time to tell the truth, my truth. And if the folks around here don't like it, and think that who I choose to sleep with, who I hand my heart to, has anything to do with how well I do my job, then so be it. I gave them the best of me, and if that still isn't good enough, then fuck all that noise. I thought I wanted to belong here. Wanted to be respected. I realize now, none of that matters if anyone else out there has to live in fear like I've done for so long. I don't want respect from people who just pick and choose which parts of me they admire. It's time I become a whole man, and if that man isn't welcome here in Sheridan, so be it."

I grabbed his chin and forced him to keep his eyes locked on mine. "Never forget, even if the man you are isn't welcome here, I want all of you, every last hang-up, all your bossy demands, your complicated history, your heroics and bravery, and even your fear and doubt. I like all your different facets and don't want you to be anyone other than who you really are when we're together. Remember that, Rodie."

This time, when he bent down to kiss me, it was not meant for an audience. There was too much teeth, too much tongue. It was wet and aggressive. The pressure and heat of his mouth on mine made my toes curl in my sneakers. I wrapped an arm around the back of his neck and held him locked to my lips, until I was forced to let go in order to catch my breath.

"Damn... now I really want to be you when I grow up, Wyatt. That was sexy as hell." Rodie and I both glared at Cam, who made a big show of fanning himself with one of Miranda's files. His dark eyes were glittering with amusement, and it was nice that he could see the humor in the situation.

"So hot." Rodie let the compliment quietly slip out and pulled away after dropping a feather-light peck to the center of my forehead. "All right. We aren't going down without a fight, so maybe we need to rally the troops and let them know what's going on, so at the very least, Cam has backup."

"We face this, and whatever else is coming our way, together." I nodded and gave Rodie a pointed look, letting him know there was no easy path before us, but that was okay.

I still had plans of my own percolating in the back of my head. I was all about Rodie dealing with the problem in a straightforward and honest way, but I liked to play with an ace up my sleeve. I wasn't letting that creep of a politician get away with threatening my lover or the young man who reminded me so much of myself. The mayor was about to find out what happened when a scrappy, homosexual kid from the swamp grew up to be a confident, well-connected, openly gay special agent. When you spent most of your life catching bad guys, and trying desperately not to become one yourself, you learned all about how to make an effective enemy.

I'd nearly killed myself to be the good guy my entire life. Now, I was going to put all those painful, regrettable lessons my mama taught me to work… all for the greater good.

CHAPTER 17

RODIE

IN ALL THE YEARS I'd been the sheriff of Sheridan, I'd never seen a turnout on a Monday night quite like this one. The high school gymnasium was packed to the point there was standing room only. It seemed like even the most remote and uninterested of the locals made the effort to drive into town for the mayor's big reveal. The curious murmurs from the crowd were almost deafening, and I couldn't stop tugging at the collar of my uniform. Nervous sweat gathered at my temples, and it took every ounce of control I possessed not to shift my weight nervously from foot to foot. I wasn't the biggest fan of public speaking on a good day, and today was anything but.

I'd dodged phone calls, threatening texts, and even more than one surprise visit from Delaney throughout the weekend, making my answer clear. I was going to take my chances with the people of Sheridan. I was willing to put what little faith I had left in the folks who had chosen me to do this job from the start. I was still incredibly worried about Cam and how the fallout from my refusal to play political games was going to affect him, but Wyatt assured me the young man was ensconced safely within the walls of the Warner compound, and no one was getting anywhere near him. I had no idea how they planned to insulate him from the gossip and speculation that was bound to explode after the mayor and Delaney dropped their fabricated evidence. I chose to believe that the love the Warners and Wyatt had for the former runaway was stronger than the hate and small-mindedness that was bound to come after the announcement. I wasn't normally a 'glass half full' type of person, but the fleeting hope was so much better than dying from thirst because you refused to put anything in the glass in the first place.

Anxiously, I scanned the gathered crowd looking for a familiar blond head. Wyatt promised he'd make an appearance tonight, knowing I was going to need the support. I caught sight of Miranda near the back of the crowded room. She shrugged somewhat helplessly when our eyes locked. She silently communicated she didn't know where Wyatt was either.

He'd been hard to pin down the last couple of days. He answered the phone when I called, though the conversations always felt rushed and brief. And he wasn't at the ranch when I stopped by after my shifts all weekend. I asked him what was going on but only got vague answers in response. I'd resorted to bugging Ten when I saw her to see if she could get any information from Webb. However, it seemed like whatever Wyatt was up to, he was keeping it to himself. No one knew what was going on with him over the weekend. All his years as an under-cover agent had obviously left him with the ability to move around secretly. He was also really good at keeping information close to the vest when he wanted to be.

"I'm surprised you showed." I jerked as a heavy hand landed on my shoulder.

I glared down at Byron Hall, my current competition and Delaney's ex-husband. He wasn't a terrible guy, but he was not the quickest on the uptake.

I shook off his hand and forced myself to uncurl my tight fists. "Didn't have a choice. The sheriff is always supposed to show up for town halls. And this close to the election, there is no way I wouldn't come."

Byron crossed his arms over his thin chest and rocked back on the heels of his cowboy boots. "Takes balls of steel to go up against Del. She can be vicious when she sets her sights on something."

I narrowed my eyes and shot the other man a cold look. "You know what she's up to?"

The other man chuckled and shook his head slowly. "No clue. But she's always up to something, and she never leaves anything to chance. You think I want to be the sheriff?" He lifted his eyebrows and snorted. "I only agreed to run against you because she backed me into a corner over a few finer details on the divorce. I never wanted to separate, and when we did, the damn woman cleaned me out. She was happy to leave me without a dime to my name. She dangled the sheriff job in front of me like a carrot on a stick. She made it seem like I couldn't say no." He stopped rocking and put his hands on his hips, looking up to meet my gaze with a serious one of his own. "She made it seem like she might consider taking me back if I managed to beat you, but seeing how desperate she is to get you out of office, I'm starting to think there's more at play here."

Maybe he wasn't as dumb as I always believed. He seemed to know there was a lot of ugly under the beautiful exterior Delaney presented to the rest of the world.

I cocked my head slightly and asked, "Do *you* think you'd make a good sheriff? Do you think you're qualified to deal with everything from homicide to chasing down escaped livestock? If I lose the position, for whatever reason, I at least want to see it go to someone who has the best interests of the town in mind."

Byron considered me thoughtfully for a minute, tilting his head as he studied me. "Why do you care about this town? I was here when you were growing up. I know for a fact you don't owe anyone in these parts anything. Seems like a waste for you to want to save them from themselves when they were ready to throw you to the wolves."

Again, I was taken aback by his rather keen observation. I lifted my chin defiantly and responded with the only reason that really mattered.

"When you decide to go into law enforcement, or the military, you're making the choice to protect and serve *everyone*. It doesn't matter what they look like, what their beliefs are, who they take to bed at night, or how they may have treated someone in the past. You're there for anyone and everyone who might need you. You're there to follow the law, which should be fair for everyone. When I look at you, I don't see you as someone who didn't do anything when we were kids and I was being bullied ruthlessly. Just like I didn't see Sutton Warner as the only friend I had had in the world back then, when all the evidence pointed to him and I had to arrest him. Following the law is easy enough, dealing with people who choose not to can be challenging. I like knowing I'm making a difference, even if the work might not be appreciated."

That was something Abe taught me. He often reminded me when I was tired, hungry, and homesick, that while people back home might not know the sacrifices the rest of my fellow soldiers and I were making for them, they got to sleep through the night unworried and safe because of the choices we made. Coming to peace with being a silent, invisible guardian angel had taken a long time, but now I fit comfortably in the role.

Byron reached out and clapped me on the shoulder once again. "Honestly, it sounds like it sucks. We both know you're the one who should be sheriff. I don't know what game Delaney is playing, but I feel like she may finally lose this one."

He could say that, but he didn't know the tricks Delaney had up her sleeve.

Our conversation was interrupted when someone tapped on a microphone; the crowd went silent as the mayor stepped up to speak first. He was dressed in a suit and had a very plastic smile plastered on his face. I wanted to put him in a chokehold and demand he learn how to be a better person so his kid had a chance at being a decent human being. Instead, all I could do was glare as the man stood in front of almost the entire town and gloated.

"Thank you all for coming tonight on such short notice. Since Sheridan is a tight, close-knit community of hard-working people who are actively involved in city government, I felt it was very important to call this town hall before the upcoming elections." He turned his head to look at me, and I rolled my eyes in response.

A moment later, all attention was pulled away from him as the doors at the back of the room crashed opened, revealing all of the Warners, and I mean *all* of them. I hadn't seen Sutton Warner since the fateful night I was forced to arrest him, but here he was along with his stunningly beautiful wife. All the brothers and their respective spouses looked ready for war, and so did Wyatt. I suddenly found myself breathing a whole lot easier now that Wyatt was in the same room. He gave me a little wink and a slight nod of encouragement that caused me to smile. It might be wishful thinking, but I now felt that everything would work out in the end, regardless of what happened tonight.

The mayor cleared his throat in annoyance, knowing good and well more attention was on the Warners' dramatic entrance than on him.

"As you know, I, as your mayor, previously endorsed Rodie Collins for the position of sheriff when we were both seeking reelection. He's held the office for several years now. I was excited to move forward with Rodie as sheriff for many more years to come, until recently when there were some troubling events here at the high school that Sheriff Collins handled questionably. I know many of you in this room are parents. And I know the rest of you are probably curious as to why my team and I suddenly switched our support to Byron Hall, who may seem less qualified for the position. I'm here tonight to explain my office's decision in full, and hope you take the information and make an informed decision when it comes time to vote."

The murmurs turned into a quiet roar, and I felt every eye in the gymnasium turn to look at me. Unspoken questions came from each and every face that was staring me down.

"What's going on at the school? Why haven't parents been notified? Does this have to do with the update to the tolerance policies?" A woman in the front row fired questions off one after another at the mayor.

He tugged on the knot of his tie. "Well, we obviously can't give the names of the children involved since they are minors."

"Bet it has to do with your kid. He's a little shit." This murmur was louder than the others and came from a middle-aged man at the back of the room. A rumbling chuckle moved through the crowd at the statement, making the mayor shift nervously.

"We aren't here because of how the children have behaved. We're here because of how the sheriff behaved. He's an adult. A public servant, just as I am. We are held to a different standard, and Sheriff Collins' actions as of late have been of some concern."

"What's he been doing?" This came from an older woman toward the front. I recognized her because I often stopped to help her scrape her windows in the winter and make sure her driveway was never blocked by the snowplows. "I see him every single day coming and going. Seems the same as always to me."

"Well…." The mayor led in, setting himself up for the big reveal.

Only, he didn't get the chance to drop his bomb, and I could see the frustration clearly on his face. He flushed a very bright red and his eyes nearly bugged out of his head when Cyrus Warner's deep voice came from the very back of the room.

"Why don't you let the sheriff explain what's been going on, since he's the reason you felt the need to sound the alarm? Rodie's always been reliable and done his job to the best of his ability. Seems a little off that all of a sudden there's a problem, and an unqualified candidate on the ballot now has your endorsement."

Because he was Cy, and because the townspeople believed him, there was a lot of demand from the audience for me to speak first. Wyatt gave me a grin and another wink, letting me know my fate was now in my own hands.

"Well, I really think you should hear what I have to say before giving Sheriff Collins the microphone." The mayor still blustered and tried to sound important, but it was clear the crowd was not in his favor. He sat behind a desk all day pushing paper. I was on the street and out in the field. These people knew what I did with my time and my position, so by default, I was the more reliable of the two of us.

I returned Wyatt's wink and made my way to the microphone. The mayor turned even redder and became more flustered when I was met with a round of applause. When he'd started the meeting, it had been nothing but silence. The situation would've been painfully awkward if it hadn't been so hilarious.

I allowed myself a small laugh as my gaze wandered over the crowd. Most of the faces were familiar, and I was surprised to see they were all watching me with expressions of curiosity and kindness. There wasn't a judgmental or angry face in the room, at least not yet.

"Hello, everyone. Thanks for taking time out of your busy schedules to show up tonight. I know I usually don't stand up and speak at these things, but tonight I feel as if I don't have a choice."

"What do you mean you don't have a choice? What in the world is going on, Sheriff?" The question came from a young father, one whom I'd helped after he'd had a car accident and was seriously injured on one of the remote ranch roads leading in and out of town.

I sighed and reached up to take off my hat. "Well, you see, the mayor and some of his staff have recently started to have a problem with me, not because of the job I'm doing for the town, but because of the man I am. The mayor didn't like the way I handled a situation between several students at the high school, and he took the initiative to have me investigated by an outside source. My service record is spotless, so he and his assistant resorted to digging into my private life to try and find something that would force me out of my job."

Uneasiness and discomfort made the entire crowd shift. I kept my gaze locked on Wyatt's blue eyes in the back of the room, because I knew the expression in them wouldn't change one bit after I said what I had to say.

"The mayor's assistant, Delaney Hall, has been aggressively pursuing me for several months. I politely and professionally turned her down repeatedly. I warned her that her actions bordered on sexual harassment, but she refused to take no for an answer."

"Men can't be sexually harassed. What kind of nonsense are you talking about, Sheriff?" The comment came from an older woman, one who looked very annoyed at being present for the town hall. "Delaney Hall is stunning and quite a catch. You should've been flattered by the attention."

My skin crawled at the response. It was what I expected to hear if I complained, but it was still disappointing and took some of the wind out of my sails. Especially when I saw the very practiced and insincere look that crossed Delaney's face at the outburst. She wasn't outright gloating, but close to it. I knew I needed to focus the attention back on the issue and not on whether or not Delaney Hall was a great catch for anyone.

"Anyone can be a victim of sexual harassment, and it doesn't matter how the aggressor looks. If the attention is unwanted and they persist, that is harassment, plain and simple. I was threatened and pressured, but I came to realize it was my fault for keeping something that is such a huge part of my life a secret that could be used against me." I let my gaze drift over the shocked faces in the room, all of them clearly dying to know what my secret was. I took a breath and plunged on. "I grew up here, as most of you know." I looked down briefly and tried to keep the bitter memories at bay. "It wasn't easy, which I think is true for a lot of us in this room. This landscape can be harsh." So could the people. "I never planned on coming back after I left the service, but fate had other plans. I started to think I was meant to be here in Sheridan all along, but the last few weeks have made me question my belief. I realized I was looking for something, had been seeking it out, but I would never find it pretending to be someone I'm not."

"What are you talking about? Is this like that twin thing that happened over at the motel a few months back?" I smiled softly at the same older woman who said I seemed normal and wondered what I could possibly be up to.

"No. This is about me being honest with myself, and the rest of you. It has nothing to do with my ability to do my job. It has absolutely no impact on any of you in this room. It isn't for the mayor or his staff to dig into. No one should have to stand in front of a crowd of people and have to declare something so personal, something so private. I'm here, about to bare my soul to you fine folks because I either tell you on my own terms, or let people with a wicked and dishonest agenda try and pull the wool over your eyes."

A few people climbed to their feet demanding answers. I saw a few bored yawns in the mix. But the majority just watched me with curious anticipation. Once again, my gaze locked on Wyatt's. The corner of his mouth kicked up in a grin. I exhaled long and slow before tapping my hat nervously against the outside of my thigh.

"I'm gay."

The silence which immediately fell over the crowd was deafening. I gulped nervously and pressed on.

"I'm not interested in Delaney Hall. I'm already involved with someone. Not the person the mayor and his assistant are going to try and convince you I'm involved with, regardless of the so-called evidence they have to back up their claims. I've never done anything I'm ashamed of in my career, as both a soldier and the sheriff of this town. I hate that I feel the need to defend myself this way, but I am left little choice. If who I choose to spend my time with off the clock is going to affect the way you vote, there is nothing I can do about it. Your choices won't affect how I go about making sure everyone in this town is protected."

This time there was no round of applause, just lots of stunned silence. I fought back a cringe as a few folks coughed uncomfortably and tried to ignore a couple of the disgusted looks thrown my way. However, no one got up and left the room, which I was going to take as a win. Stepping away from the microphone, I put my hat back on my head and bowed my head ever so slightly.

As I stepped back to the side of the area where the mayor and Byron were waiting, I noticed that Wyatt was purposefully making his way through the crowd. Initially, I thought he was coming toward me to offer support so we could make a stand together, but as he reached me, he bypassed me altogether. Wyatt marched right up to the mayor who was waiting anxiously to take the microphone back from one of his aides, trying to regain control of the suddenly wild room. Wyatt put a hand on the mayor's chest and lowered his head, speaking in a tone so low I couldn't overhear anything he was saying, but the look on the mayor's face was alarmed. This definitely had my interest piqued.

"I have something to say."

My head whipped around as Byron Hall's voice abruptly filled the gym. I'd been so focused on Wyatt, I missed the other man moving forward.

"When I agreed to run against Rodie, I didn't have all the facts. My ex-wife made it sound like a good idea, and repeatedly told me Rodie wasn't following through on his job commitments. I never wanted to be the sheriff. I'm a businessman and a rancher. I know livestock better than I know the law. I allowed the mayor to convince me that running for sheriff make sense, when it absolutely doesn't. There isn't a better person for the job than Rodie Collins. I'm officially dropping out of the running, so if you aren't going to vote for him because of who he loves, it won't matter. All he needs is one vote to win when running unopposed, and he has mine, hands down."

I felt my mouth gape open in shock as I stared at the other man. Byron nodded slightly, and tilted his head toward the stirring crowd.

"He has my vote, as well." Cy's deep booming voice echoed through the room.

"Mine, too." Leo's chipper voice soon followed, along with a little finger wave as she stood up on her tippy toes to be seen through the crowd.

"Mine, as well." I was shocked when Lane took a step forward, soon followed by Brynn and Ten, who echoed his sentiment.

My gaze found my former best friend's and I watched as Sutton lifted a blond brow. "I don't live here any longer, but if I did, I'd vote for him. Rodie is the most honest, trustworthy person I've ever met, and he genuinely cares about each and every single person in this room. Don't be stupid and start looking at him any differently than you always have. He's the exact same person as he was before the mayor dragged us into his bedroom."

I exhaled so hard I was sure it could be heard at the back of the room. I felt my eyes go wide as other people in the crowd suddenly started getting to their feet and declaring I still had their vote and would until it was my choice to leave the office.

Of course, not everyone was so supportive. I heard several whispered homophobic slurs, and both the dad I helped in the accident and the older rancher who spoke first got up to leave without looking back, but the majority didn't seem to care one way or the other about my announcement. It was so much more than I could ask for. It was a startling relief and so unexpected, I felt my knees start to wobble.

Luckily, Wyatt reappeared at my side, sliding an arm around my waist, and put his palm on my lower back to keep me upright. The remaining crowd murmured like the last piece of the puzzle had clicked into place. Without thinking about it too much, I leaned into him, hoping we both wouldn't end up in a tangle of limbs on the ground since he wasn't holding his cane.

"Went better than expected." There was a hint of laughter in his voice.

"It isn't over yet. They still have those pictures." Which meant they could drag Cam into this whole mess as a patsy for revenge any time they wanted.

Wyatt's fingers tapped my back and a crooked grin crossed his handsome face. "Don't worry about that anymore. Take this win, and decide what you want to do next."

There was something in his tone that sent chills up my spine. I pulled away slightly and gave him a hard look from under the brim of my hat. "What are you up to, pretty boy?"

Chuckling under his breath, he reached up and tapped my chin with his forefinger. "Now would be the time for you to call me 'Special Agent' instead." He stepped back and wiggled his eyebrows. "It's time to celebrate. I'll tell you what I dug up later."

I'd wondered what he'd been up to when he was acting so secretive all weekend. I felt like he ignored me when I said I didn't want to sink to the mayor and Delaney's level.

Apparently, seeing the disapproval on my face, he once again reached up and tapped my chin, this time pausing so he could brush his thumb over the curve of my lower lip. "Don't worry, Sheriff. I didn't break any laws, and I didn't find anything anyone else wouldn't if they bothered to look. Just trust me on this one."

"He's even prettier than Delaney Hall." Wyatt and I both jerked around as the elderly woman whose driveway I cleared ambled by. "And I'd say you look just as good with him as you would with her. Better even, because he actually makes you smile. I know you had a hard road in these parts as a kid, Rodie. But you made your way back, better than ever, and that means something around here."

She gave us a pert little nod and merged with the rest of the crowd leaving through the back doors. The mayor and Delaney had their heads bent together and were whispering furiously, glancing over in Wyatt's direction every so often. Byron was standing off to the side with an entirely pleased look on his face. I owed the man a lot. I was going to have to thank him and let him know I owed him a big ass favor down the road.

"Let's get out of here." Wyatt's voice turned husky, and the look in his eyes went heated and intent. "I feel like you deserve a reward for facing your biggest fear in front of everyone."

"What kind of reward?" I already knew and my body was ready.

Wyatt chuckled and tilted his chin back defiantly. "Whatever you want."

That left the door open for a lot of interpretation.

I wondered if he was ready to hear that what I wanted most was for him to agree to stay. Not necessarily in Sheridan — but with me — no matter where that may be in the future.

CHAPTER 18

WYATT

I WAS SURPRISED BY THE interior of Rodie's home. I was expecting a barren, bachelor vibe similar to the condo I sold in DC not too long ago. I wasn't expecting something chic you could easily find on any HGTV show. There were soft colors painted on the walls and modern furniture that looked like something out of a magazine. For a man who lived in faded jeans and cowboy boots, there was a lot of style splattered around. It went all the way to the bedroom, where Rodie crowded me without offering a tour of his smallish home. He tried to pry the information I scraped together about the mayor out of me on our short trip to his place, but I didn't want to distract from the victory he'd had at the town hall. He needed a moment to absorb the fact that he'd faced his biggest fear and came out on the other side relatively unscathed.

Grinning as he used his big, strong body to back me toward the large bed in the center of the room, I lifted an eyebrow and asked, "Did you hire a decorator? I have a hard time believing a guy like you knows what wainscoting is."

I landed with a slight exclamation, the soft mattress at my back. Rodie hovered over me, one of his hands planted above my head as he braced a knee on the bed next to my hip. I was effectively caged in, and I wasn't going to complain about it. I was done trying to get away.

"This was the first place I ever lived that I got to call my own. I'd never lived anywhere that was entirely mine, so I spent a lot of time on it."

Once again, he was showing me how badly I'd failed at moving past all the things in life that had left their mark. I'd owned my place in DC, but was rarely there since I was always working. The condo felt more like a high-end hotel than a home, even though I told myself all I wanted in life was a place to call my own without the memories of my childhood haunting every corner. All I ended up with was an expensive box that felt as cold and sterile as all the places I bounced around when I was younger.

I didn't get to think about his decorating acumen any longer because my attention was stolen by a steamy kiss that was all lips and tongue. It was a great distraction from the décor, but there was still something pressing I wanted to get off my chest. I turned my head when Rodie slanted his mouth in the opposite direction, trying to steal my breath and blow my mind from another angle.

I grabbed his face between my hands and held him still. I made sure his gaze was locked on mine before I quietly told him, "I'm really proud of you, ya know?"

His green eyes flared, turning a brighter shade. A touch of pink crossed his high cheekbones, and the corner of his usually stern mouth lifted lightly.

"It's hard to be open and honest with the people closest to you without knowing the reaction you might get. I can't imagine what it felt like to come out to an entire community the way you did. That was brave, and sexy as hell." I smiled back at him. I knew mine held a hint of sadness. "You kept saying you were hiding, but you really weren't. You were living your life under the radar, tucked away in the closet because it was safe for you in there. You were minding your own business because you were afraid to let anyone in, because you'd been hurt by those who were supposed to care about you. Anyone would be leery after that. I was the one hiding in plain sight. When went undercover, I got to be someone else. Someone without my past. Someone without my problems. I got to play pretend for real, which meant I never had to face the issues I'd spent an eternity denying. I think part of the reason I couldn't accept the desk job, and why I've been struggling so hard since leaving the DEA, is because now I have to be me. I have to learn to live as Wyatt Bryant, no one else, and I'm not sure how to go about doing that."

Rodie watched me for a long moment before dropping his head and placing a playful kiss on the end of my nose.

"I don't know how to live as an open and honest Rodie Collins either. We can figure it out together and navigate the unexpected detours hand in hand."

Shockingly, I didn't mind the sound of that at all. It was different kind of challenge and adventure than I was used to, but it would keep me on my toes just as much as my old life had.

He kissed me again, so I whispered against his lips, "I owe you a reward. Tell me what you want, Sheriff."

His green eyes glittered like emeralds, and the smile on his face turned seductive and slightly sinister.

"Oh, I can think of a few things I want, pretty boy, but for tonight, all I want is for you to do anything I ask." His dark eyebrows danced upward, and his teeth flashed wickedly.

"Anything?" That was pretty broad and sounded like it could be a whole lot of fun.

"Whatever I tell you to do, you have to comply. If you're good and do what I say, then you'll earn your own reward. Are you up for it?"

I wasn't surprised he had a dominant streak that slipped out when clothes started coming off and walls started coming down. It wasn't something I'd normally be attracted to in a partner, but it was part of his personality, so I didn't mind it. In fact, I kind of liked it. I always had a hard time turning off the whirling thoughts in my head, even during sex. Somehow, when I was following Rodie's lead and leaning into the deep, husky voice telling me what he liked, all of that extra, annoying noise simply went away.

"Do your worst." A chuckle followed the words as he kissed me again.

"No. With you, Wyatt, I'll always do my best." His rasp was even sexier when he was making promises like that.

The kiss went wild, teeth clicking together as he used his free hand to start unbuttoning my shirt. I followed suit, helping him out of the uniform shirt and going to work on the massive belt buckle he always wore. Anticipation made my skin tingle and my blood buzz. I waited breathlessly for whatever he was going to ask me to do first. Not knowing what was coming upped the intensity of the feelings and emotions coursing through me.

We undressed in silence, the sound of descending zippers and labored breathing loud in the room. It occurred to me it was the middle of the day and I'd never done anything before as bold and wanton with the sun shining. Yet another new thing Rodie was leading me into. I never realized how much I'd repressed in my life because of the lingering fear of being hurt, at least until he opened my eyes.

Between biting kisses and grabbing hands, I was breathless and fighting the urge to squirm underneath him. I felt the damp tip of his cock drag along the sensitive skin of my inner thigh. The contact made my own erection twitch eagerly and forced my hips to lift off the bed.

Rodie's eyes gleamed, and he caught my restless hands in one of his, pinning them to the bed above my head.

"Leave those there."

The first order made me suck in a deep breath and I felt my face flush. My heart kicked hard, and goosebumps broke out across my skin. I stilled and watched with wide eyes as he switched his attention from my mouth to other parts of my body.

His lips skated down the side of my neck, and he nibbled on my collar bone. He kissed his way down the center of my chest, stopping to use his teeth on one of my nipples. The sting curled my hands into fists and I had to really concentrate on not moving them. He switched to the other side, using his lips and tongue instead; the contrast between the little bit of pain and the soft caress made me groan. I felt his heated length press against mine, making my balls tight and the rigid shaft between my legs pulse in response. Rodie muttered something that sounded approving, and his tongue danced across the corrugated lines of my abs, the tip detouring to dip into the tiny indent of my belly button.

I couldn't stop my hips from lifting, chasing the sweet sensation. Rodie lifted his head, the pleased grin on his face stealing my breath and making me shiver.

"Turn over." The command was rough and I could see a slight tremor making the muscles in his arms twitch.

I gulped, debating if I had the balls to be so open and vulnerable in broad daylight. Rodie watched patiently as I slowly pulled my head and heart together and did as he requested.

My hands curled tightly into the sheets, and my breath wheezed out when I felt his lips touch the top of my spine. One of his wandering hands landed on my backside and gave the firm globe a squeeze. I closed my eyes and let the sensation swamp me as his tongue glided down the entire length of my back. My shoulders stiffened and I felt my cock start to rapidly swell and leak onto the sheets underneath me. The friction was enough to distract from what Rodie was doing, but the dual stimulation was enough that pops of bright light burst behind my eyelids.

"Get on your knees."

I automatically complied, shifting underneath him restlessly when I felt the warmth of his breath across the top curve of my ass. It didn't even occur to me that I'd made so much progress during physical therapy the last few weeks that I could get into the familiar position without too much of my body protesting. It was a good thing I really did act like a Boy Scout and keep myself always prepared, because it would've been a real shame to tell him to stop in the middle of something that felt so damn good.

The sound that burst out of me at the first swipe of his tongue against that sensitive, tender hole sounded almost inhuman. I panted loudly, trying not to push my ass into his face and focus instead on getting one of my hands around my throbbing, neglected cock.

"Hey."

I protested weakly when Rodie caught my wandering hand and held it still. I grumbled louder when he lifted his head and told me, "No touching until I tell you."

So far, I'd liked what he told me to do. My aching, pulsing cock wasn't too happy with this one. It hung heavy between my legs, the tip shiny and slick with precum.

A second later I forgot to be frustrated because Rodie was back to flicking his tongue against my puckered hole, taking his time until it fluttered open and he could spear the tip inside.

I swallowed a moan, hips shifting, seeking more contact, chasing more pleasure. I felt hot all over and swore that each and every heartbeat was making my cock thump in time. All I wanted was to wrap my hand around the aching shaft and find some relief. Rodie must've known he was making me suffer, because his chuckle vibrated against my most sensitive spot. I swore I was on the brink of coming with zero contact to my cock, which would absolutely be a first for me.

Once everything was wet and slippery, and I was a quaking, writhing mess on the bed in front of him, I felt the bite of his teeth on one flexed butt cheek and Rodie lifted his head.

"I want you to ride me." He rasped out the words, hands shaking as he stroked my spine.

I blinked my eyes open and turned to look at him over my shoulder. "Is that an order?"

He laughed again, and I realized when he was happy, he was probably the best-looking man I had ever laid eyes on.

"Ride me." His voice was firm and the gleam in his eyes made my cock jump once again.

"What if I want you to ride me as my reward?" We'd never really had the conversation about how open he was to reversing the roles we'd played thus far.

His dark eyebrows quirked, and his smile once again went slightly naughty. "All you have to do is ask, Special Agent."

My breath escaped in a loud *whoosh*, and if it was possible, my cock got even harder.

"Duly noted. I'm going to ask." I barely got the words out around all the emotion lodged in my throat. I gasped when I felt cool liquid hit the already over-sensitized hole he'd been playing with.

"Can't wait."

I never knew it could be this easy.

Imagine if I'd never found him. If I'd never stopped moving and pretending. I would have missed out on so much.

Rodie shifted our positions, the bed moving and dipping under his weight. Instead of straddling and facing him, he ordered me to face the other way. It was that same disconnect when I couldn't touch myself. It amped up each and every move, every touch, every breath. It was like being balanced on the edge of something very high up, waiting for someone to push you off. I hadn't felt this kind of thrill since I walked away from my job.

It did something to my insides to know Rodie could read me so well. I had no idea how he figured out the tiny tingle of suspense made everything we did to each other so much better.

He handled the protection, but once again stopped me from reaching for my dick. I growled at him in a threatening manner, pulling a deep laugh from his wide chest. He knew he was torturing me, and was getting off on it.

A moment later his big hands were on my hips as I carefully hovered over his straining erection. We both gasped when the tapered head breached my small opening. Since he was keeping me hanging, I took my time working his full length inside. Only, he was too good at finding the spot that drove me wild and made me forget to have any kind of composure. Pleasure almost instantly exploded across all my nerve endings, and desire took over. All I could do was beg for more and move frantically on top of him.

Rodie hummed in appreciation, shifting underneath me. Everywhere we touched was burning hot, pulsing with its own kind of life and electricity.

Rodie growled my name, his strong fingers digging into my hips with enough force to leave marks. All my attention was focused on my cock, I swear I could hear it howling, demanding some kind of pressure and stimulation. My insides clenched and flexed around Rodie's unrelenting flesh as I got ready to disobey his command, not caring about the consequences.

I swore at him, eyes nearly rolling back in my head from the onslaught of pleasure. I heard his breath catch and felt his hips kick erratically. I knew he was close to losing it before he told me he was. I was going to kill him a second after he came if he kept me on the edge.

About a second before I felt the pulse and rush of his release, he barked, "Touch yourself, Wyatt," and I almost sobbed with relief.

As soon as my palm touched my heated skin, everything exploded in an intense rush. My eyes slammed closed, my lungs seized, my skin felt like it came alive, and my mind went totally blank. I came with enough force that it felt like I might black out. It felt so good, it was almost painful.

I nearly collapsed on top of Rodie as soon as the last bit of liquid surged out of the glistening tip.

I moaned and bent forward so I could rest my forehead against one of his knees. I wanted to die, then come back to life and do this exact same thing all over again. It was that good.

I exhaled and knocked my forehead playfully against the hard surface. "You're dangerous, Sheriff."

He hummed again, hands going to my ass. I felt him press against the tensed cheeks so he could look at the point where we were still connected.

"I have something else I want to tell you to do since you have to listen to me, but instead, I'm going to ask." For the first time since I'd met him, he sounded hesitant and unsure.

I lifted up and looked at him over my shoulder, shuddering as it pushed his softening erection back into my tender entrance.

"What do you want to ask me?" There were a million things it could be, and if I wasn't sex-drunk and caught in a spiral of satisfaction, I would've been picking each one of them apart.

He cleared his throat and reached up to trace a random pattern across my shoulders. It took me a minute to realize he was drawing a heart with our initials. It was a surprisingly sweet gesture from such a stern man, and it almost guaranteed I was going to agree to anything. I was shocked at the submissive side that came to the forefront with this man.

"Stay with me. I don't want you to go." The admission was shaky and a little sad, as if he assumed I already had an answer.

We watched each other silently for a long moment. Rodie had his heart in his eyes and I could see he was waiting for me to break it.

Instead, I whispered, "Tell me to stay." I couldn't say no.

His eyebrows shot upward and his mouth dropped open before he burst out, "Don't go."

I lifted up, separating us and making us both moan. I turned around so I was facing him, and I put a hand on his chest where I could feel his heart pounding.

"I'm not going anywhere."

It was the first time I'd ever said those words. It was the first time I'd found a place I wanted to stay, and the first time I'd met someone I couldn't leave behind.

CHAPTER 19

RODIE

"**W**HAT DID YOU SAY to the mayor at the town hall?" There was a lot to process at the moment. The unreal sex. The fact Wyatt said he wasn't going anywhere. Knowing my job wasn't immediately in danger once the town really knew who they were voting for. And the message that just came across my phone from one of my deputies: the mayor had suddenly pulled his name from the election. With no rhyme or reason, and no explanation, all the gossip in town was now centered around him instead of me.

Wyatt stretched his arms above his head and let out a yawn. His blue eyes looked sleepy and sexy, but the smirk on his face was smug and had me even more intrigued.

"I told him it would be a good idea for him to drop out of the election if he didn't want anyone to find out that he was scamming the town."

I felt my eyebrows twitch as I pushed up so my back was resting against the headboard. "I thought I told you to leave it alone." I should've known he was going to ignore my request. The man couldn't stand by and watch an injustice happen. It just wasn't in his wiring.

"You told me not to play dirty, and I didn't. I looked into some of the promises the mayor made during his campaigns, and some things didn't add up. I know a couple agents at the Colorado Bureau of Investigation from when they were investigating Webb, and asked around to see if there were any complaints lodged against him. They managed to dig up information in places I can't access any longer. When you hate an entire group of people for no reason, it follows that you're probably prejudiced against others, as well. The mayor made repeated promises to fund various scholarships and education programs for children on the reservations surrounding Sheridan. It was a repeated message in all of his campaigns and a key talking point of his fundraising initiatives. Good, honest people gave him money thinking he was going to help those kids.

"Do you think anyone on any of the reservations around this town have seen a dime?"

He rolled over in the tangled sheets and braced his head on one of his hands, watching me carefully.

"He took that money and did Lord only knows with it. Various groups from the reservations lodged complaints about never seeing any improvement in the education systems, but no one ever took action because the mayor kept insisting he was putting together a special task force. Marginalized voices often get overlooked like this. People are far too conditioned to turn a blind eye to those in need of a little bit more love and support. But now I know, and you know, and soon this entire town will know about it. Hopefully something good will come from that bigoted asshole going up against us."

I rubbed a hand down my face, disappointed, but not surprised by this information. "You managed to find all of that out in two days?" And he said *I* was dangerous. It was a good reminder that Wyatt was so much more than a pretty face. The man was a formidable opponent and could be downright scary in the right circumstances. How lucky was I? He even said the mayor had gone up against *us*. I had no idea such a tiny little word could take up so much room inside my heart.

Wyatt chuckled. "I just asked some questions and made myself a nuisance until I got answers. I'm sorry I was late to the town hall. But it was worth it to put that idiot in his place."

"I wasn't sure I was going to be able to go through with it until I saw you." I was being honest. My determination wavered when it came time to face my ultimate fear, but knowing he was there, that I could rely on him no matter the fallout, made a huge difference.

He reached up and dragged the tip of a finger down the bridge of my nose. I was going to get addicted to the casual, confident way he showed simple affection. As someone who had been denied basic human contact and warmth throughout my formative years, the way he put his hands on me meant everything.

"You would've been fine, even if I wasn't there. I knew you wouldn't let Cam get caught up in that nonsense. I didn't doubt for a second that you would sacrifice yourself to save him. You're a really good guy, Rodie. If you weren't, I don't think I would have considered what life would be like if I stuck around Sheridan." He tapped the end of my nose and rolled over onto his back. He crossed his hands behind his head as he stared up at the ceiling. "It'll be interesting to see who steps up to take the mayor's place now that the position is about to be vacant. Hopefully it'll be someone more open-minded, someone looking to represent every type of resident Sheridan has."

I reached out so I could ruffle his messy hair. The strands felt like silk between my fingers. "What about you? You're gonna have to find something to do with your free time if you're staying. You can't be unemployed forever." I was just teasing him. I would gladly let him stay at home and support him if that was how things were going to play out.

Wyatt leaned into the slight caress, vibrant eyes sliding closed in contentment. "I'm not cut out for politics. Too many rules, too many people breaking them for their own objectives. But I have been giving a lot of thought to what my future should look like."

"Oh yeah? What does it look like?" As long as there was a place for me in it, the details didn't really matter to me. I would stand by him regardless. Like he'd just done for me.

"I think it looks bright, maybe even happy. I'm not sure, because I've never really seen things that way before." He blinked up at me and flashed a shy smile. "Webb and Ten bought a huge piece of land with the dirty money my worthless father left for him. They're going to build a house, and Webb asked me to put some roots down right next to him. I don't think I'm ready to be so close to my little brother all the time, but it got me thinking. I wasn't planning on touching the money from our father. I didn't want anything to do with it, or him. But there are so many people out there the money could help, it's selfish for me to keep pretending like it doesn't exist. How can I justify ignoring kids like Cam, who have no one and nowhere to go? Or those kids on the reservation who get overlooked and forgotten. A little attention and financial backing can go such a long way."

I made a soft sound of agreement as I continued to pet him. "Not just kids like Cam. Kids like you and Webb, too. There is no reason for any child to be tossed out on the streets, starving and desperate."

He turned his head slightly, blue eyes blazing with deep emotion. "And kids like you, who feel like they have no one who understands them, no one to rely on. You may have had a roof over your head, but it was just as cold inside those four walls as it was for us when we had to sleep on the ground." He cleared his throat and gave a little nod. "I want to help kids who need it. Webb has been learning the dude ranch business from Cyrus and Lane. I've been thinking about some kind of camp, or some kind of retreat for LGBTQ kids. Some kind of safe haven for those marginalized voices. I want them to know they are seen and heard. I want them to know someone out there cares. We can give them a roof over their heads, three square meals a day, life skills training, and even therapy. I was hoping I could talk to Cyrus and Leo about it. I think if I can figure out a solid business plan, I could convince the Warners to partner with me and Webb on the project down the road."

It was clear the idea had been percolating for a while. He spoke with confidence and assurance, as if he'd finally figured out his true calling. I wasn't at all surprised his endgame was to help others who were in deep need. We both had the driving desire to make sure no one else went through the things we did when we were younger. Our childhoods sucked, but there was no denying they'd helped turn us into the compassionate men we were today. We suffered so others wouldn't have to. He was the one who was a really good guy.

"So, you were planning on staying before I asked?" I was happy it meant I got to keep him and got more time with him, but if I was being honest, I was a little let down I hadn't been part of his deciding factor. I wanted to be as important to him as he was to me.

Wyatt moved so fast I almost forgot he was still healing from some serious injuries. I was manhandled back to the mattress, and ended up with a big, blond former special agent propped on top of me, pinning me to the bed. Blue eyes blazed into mine, and his pretty features were set into fierce lines.

"I wanted to stay, but I was looking for a reason. Watching you go to bat for Cam, knowing you were going to stop living in the dark, made up my mind for me. I knew I wasn't going to be able to walk away when you came out to the town. There was no way I was leaving you alone to deal with that. When I realized I couldn't leave you behind, it got me thinking about what I was going to do with myself in the middle of nowhere. You inspired me, Rodie. Don't ever doubt it."

"Good to know." He inspired me, too. He made me want more than just a paycheck and a place to call home.

We were both still naked, so the fact he was on top of me, and the way he was handling me, forced my body to respond almost instantly. My dick got hard, and I felt his swell and lengthen against my stomach. The intensity of his gaze took on a new dimension, and the way he was holding me down switched to something else in the span of a second. His hands went from pressing down on my shoulders to skimming across my chest and brushing across my nipples. I sucked in a sharp breath through my teeth and arched my neck when he lowered his head to kiss his way across my jaw.

I was usually the aggressor, not that I was complaining about Wyatt stepping up to take the lead. As much as I appreciated his submissive side, I liked when he got fierce and demanding. It wasn't often I was with someone who could give as good as I gave. It was another sign Wyatt really might be the perfect man for me. I wasn't sure what I'd done to deserve him, but I was sure happy with my reward.

And he seemed pretty happy with his.

He shifted his hips, pressing his erection more firmly against my stomach. His teeth latched onto my ear as his quick fingers returned to the sensitive points on my chest. Muscles flexed and tightened as breaths quickened and blood heated. We weren't teenagers any longer, so we shouldn't be amped up and recovering this quickly after that energetic round of sex we'd just had, but it seemed like none of the old rules were going to apply to us when we were together.

All it took was a few wet, hungry kisses, and the brush of eager hands over hard flesh to have us both panting and subtly grinding against one another. I was waiting for him to turn the tables on me. I was slightly breathless, waiting for him to start telling me what he wanted me to do, but the demands and orders never came. Instead, he seduced me silently with his lips and hands. Before I knew what was happening, I was a quivering, shaking mess of anticipation underneath him, wordlessly begging for him to put me out of my misery.

He held our cocks together in one wide palm and slowly worked them up and down. He was very good at stimulating both of us at the same time, so I closed my eyes and sank into the sensation. I felt his teeth on the side of my neck and realized he was marking me the same way I'd marked him. We were declaring ownership of each other, and nothing in my life felt as significant as this singular moment. I'd never had anyone to call my own. And more importantly, I'd never had anyone step up and do the work required to call me theirs.

In the heat of the moment earlier, he said he was going to ask me to ride him, so I shifted restlessly waiting for him to put the words into action. Instead, Wyatt brought us both to the very edge of completion with just his hands and mouth. Right when I was about to burst out of my skin and order him to finish us off, he suddenly moved between my spread legs. My eyebrows shot up in surprise. In all my years as sexually active adult, I couldn't recall a time I'd ever made love with someone face to face. Regardless of my position during the most intimate of moments, facing whomever I was with in the dark made me feel far too vulnerable and exposed.

There was none of that with Wyatt. He saw through any mask I tried to wear, and I'd never managed to keep a single secret from him. He saw right through me from the start, so I had no trouble looking him right in those beautiful blue eyes as he moved my legs where he wanted them to get both of us ready.

My body twitched and softened around his probing fingers. My dick throbbed in anticipation as pleasure coiled tightly at the base of my spine. Wyatt took his time, and he was careful with the way he stroked me. He was good at reading my body language, but he was fixed on my eyes. He must have been able to see how close I was to losing it, because right before I came all over my own hand, he pressed inside of my very ready opening. All it took was that first stretch and give of interior flesh and muscle for pleasure to explode inside of me. Normally, I'd be embarrassed about being so quick on the trigger, but Wyatt was right behind me. It only took a few hurried thrusts and my body instinctively clamping down on his for him to groan my name and collapse in a satisfied heap on top of me.

We were quiet in the aftermath because words weren't needed.

Nothing more was needed.

Here, in the middle of nowhere, we had it all and then some.

We were going to do great things together… for ourselves, and for others.

If anyone told me I would have to go back to the very beginning where I thought it all went wrong to find everything that was right, I never would have believed them. And just like I'd sold this place to Abe when I was convinced I hated it, I was going to move forward with Wyatt. I would make sure others who needed to heal knew this place was special. They had a place here among people who genuinely cared about them.

Under the wide open, pristine sky, wonderful things managed to happen. I could see them all now.

EPILOGUE

THREE YEARS LATER

I WAS EXHAUSTED WHEN I finally got back to the small house in the center of town I'd called home since I'd moved in with Rodie a couple years ago. My younger brother was still holding out hope I would change my mind and build a bigger place on the compound that now included a fully operating halfway house for all sorts of displaced youth. However, I liked Rodie's immaculately decorated house. I appreciated the time and care he put into creating something of his own. I liked that it was actually located in Sheridan and not on the outskirts of everything. It meant well-meaning friends and family couldn't just drop in whenever they wanted, which was also nice. I hadn't given up my mile-wide independent streak just because I was now surrounded by people who loved me unconditionally. While I would never fully adjust to the quiet and lack of smog and traffic, I was slowly getting used to small-town living.

I'd been out at the property Webb cheerfully dubbed Runaway Ranch late this evening. We'd gotten a new group of kids and they'd been delayed due to the weather. Webb and I waited until they were all warmed up, fed properly, and situated in the space before going over the rules and regulations of the property. Often times, the kids balked when they heard about the strict requirements, one of which was daily counseling, in order to stay at the ranch, and it took us hours to convince them to stay. Such was the case tonight. There was a young man, probably around the same age Cam had been when he came to Wyoming, who was absolutely defiant and ready to leave as soon as he arrived. I knew a lot of the kids had never had anyone reach out and try and help them before, so they didn't know what to do with the kindness and care when there was suddenly an abundant supply of it.

We never forced anyone to stay, but we refused to put them in danger, so they couldn't go anywhere until the weather was better. Fortunately, the young man this evening eventually calmed down and agreed to sleep on his decision to leave. I was relieved, but the drive back to my own home took a lot longer than normal, and by the time I walked in the door, I was dead on my feet.

Rodie called twice to make sure I was okay on the drive, but I could hear how tired he was, as well. There had been a series of sexual assaults across the county over the last few months, and both Rodie and Ten had been handpicked to be part of the taskforce investigating the crimes. He had a lot going on. We both did. But there was one reason we both made it home every single night, no matter what.

That reason was currently curled up in her crib, one thumb tucked into her pouty little mouth, looking like a perfect little doll as she dreamed. I reached out a finger and touched her baby soft cheek, fighting back the sting of tears as she curled into the touch and cooed adorably.

I'd always wanted kids, wanted the dream idea of what a family was supposed to look like, but it never seemed like it was something I was going to have. Then Rodie Collins burst into my life, all flirty and ferocious, and suddenly nothing seemed impossible. Because families could look like anything as long as they had love.

At the beginning of the year, we'd taken in a young girl. A girl too young to live on the streets. A girl far too young to sell her body to survive. A girl way too innocent to have first-hand knowledge of what it was like to be used and abused by someone older. A girl too young to be responsible for a baby. She was a sweet kid who felt like her life was over and that she'd reached the end of her rope. I was terrified she was going to end her own life and take the life growing inside of her, too. It was one of the most complicated cases we'd faced since opening the ranch.

Luckily, she pulled through with a lot of help from our staff psychiatrist and support from other kids who had faced similarly horrible experiences. Knowing she wasn't alone, and that she wasn't the only one going through something so traumatic, pulled her through. Before the baby came, she pulled me aside and asked me to look into adoption options for her. Excited she was fighting to keep living for herself and her baby, I readily agreed. I hadn't planned on Rodie suggesting that he and I adopt the baby. At first, I believed he was just being his typical problem-solver self, but he persisted, and once he put the idea in my head, I couldn't let it go. We spoke to the young woman, making sure she had the support she needed in the event she wanted to turn us down. Only, she'd been ecstatic at the idea and had promptly burst into tears, claiming she wished we could adopt her, as well. While taking on an emotionally distraught teen and a baby at the same time would prove challenging, Rodie and I determined we were up to the challenge. The fact that he didn't even blink when I suggested taking both of them in solidified that he was the only man I was ever going to love and want to share a home and family with. After the baby came and papers were signed, and all the legal mumbo-jumbo was out of the way, the baby's mother decided she didn't want to stay in Wyoming. I found a lovely foster family in Florida willing to take her in. She left, but we all agreed to keep the adoption open so she could always come back if she wanted a relationship with her daughter.

Now I was a father, and so was Rodie. Little Eliana had only changed our lives for the better. During the day, she usually came to work with me and was doted on by the entire staff at the ranch, as well as all her aunts and uncles. Webb loved her like she was his own and claimed he didn't need to worry about having his own kids because he was just going to help raise mine. Ten seemed on board with that plan, claiming the kids at the ranch were enough for her. Rodie came and got the baby when he was off shift, and if he couldn't watch her and I was still working, Miranda was the best grandmother Eliana could ask for. She played a huge part in helping us take care of the baby, and Rodie insisted his former CO was somewhere watching us all thrive with a smile on his face. The attractive older woman had even been open to the idea of dating more recently, so we were all rooting for her to have her own happy ever after.

"Hey." I turned at the sleepy sound of Rodie's voice behind me. He looked as tired as I felt, but it didn't make him any less attractive. He was finally starting to get some white and silver streaks in his reddish hair, but it looked good on him. So did the soft smile that automatically crossed his face when the baby cooed again.

"She was fussy tonight. I think she was worried about you." He put a hand on the back of my neck and gave it a gentle squeeze.

I sighed and let my eyes fall closed. "It was a long day. I'm glad she was with Leo today. The ranch turned to utter chaos once it started snowing."

"Ahh... I forgot Mayor Warner took her from Miranda today to spend some time with the twins." He yawned loudly, then peeked at the baby to make sure he didn't wake her up. "She's lucky to have so many people who love her."

I nodded in agreement and turned to usher him out of the artfully decorated nursery. "So are we." So lucky to have so much love in all corners of our life.

When the mayor dropped out of the race years ago, the local government was up in the air for a long time. The town buzzed for months after the news of the former mayor's mishandling of city funds came to light. Things were so bad that the mayor moved his entire family out of town, which was a win on many levels, and ensured the rest of Cam's high school days would be much easier.

For a while, I pressured Rodie to press charges against Delaney Hall for sexual harassment her role in how everything went down. I was furious she managed to keep her job and remained unscathed by the mayor's unfolding scandal. Rodie claimed he wanted to let sleeping dogs lie. As long as Delaney didn't try to drag Cam through the mud and release the misleading photos, he was content to let her be. He really wanted to protect the teenager unwittingly caught up in the whole mess. I wasn't as willing to let things go. Just like I had with the mayor, I devoted some time to digging deeply into Delaney's past. The skeletons in her closet were better hidden, but I'd eventually managed to find a few.

First and foremost, Rodie wasn't the only male coworker she'd made uncomfortable with her aggressive advances. I'd tracked no less than three other men who mentioned how awful it'd been to work with her. When I pressed them all about pressing charges, no one wanted the stigma attached to a man being sexually harassed. They were afraid that no one would believe them and they'd lose face. They were worried about how a lawsuit against a pretty, successful young woman would affect their current careers and relationships. It forced me to see Rodie's side of the situation a little more clearly. Secondly, it wasn't only surveillance photos she liked to collect. When it was time to play dirty to get the dirt, I had a fed buddy hack into her computer and was very alarmed at what was uncovered. There were hundreds of pictures of teenage boys in various stages of undress in compromising positions with Delaney. The mayor's son was one of them. In the end, Delaney served a harsher punishment than the mayor, who was slapped on the wrist and ordered to pay back the money he took from the scholarship fund. After a short investigation, she was arrested by the same fed who helped me hack her computer on child pornography charges. She was still awaiting trial, but things didn't look good for her. She was finally in a situation she couldn't use money or her looks to get herself out of.

It wasn't until the following year that, Leo, Cyrus's spitfire wife, decided to step up and take control of the situation. She was a surprisingly good choice, even though she wasn't a lifelong resident of Sheridan. The pretty redhead had a savvy business mind from her years as a corporate executive, and she really understood the needs of the people in Sheridan after running Cy's ranch with him for several years. The townsfolk loved her, and she was elected by a landslide. After being in office for a month, she announced she was pregnant with twins. The little boys were slightly older than Eliana, but the entire Warner clan treated them all as if they were siblings. It was easy, considering the rapid pace the entire brood was growing.

Sutton and Emrys had added another little girl to their family out in California, but now all of them came home to Wyoming in the summers to spend time with the family. Daye, possibly the sassiest young lady alive, adored being the oldest of the group and being the boss of all the babies. She was a pro at being the big sister, and Cam had slowly adapted to being everyone's big brother. Much like Ten and Webb, who had decided to give their love and attention to kids from outside the family, Lane and Brynn opted to wait on having children of their own and instead focused on building a family full of kids who needed them. Along with formally adopting Cam, they'd also taken in two young sisters from the reservation where Brynn grew up after their parents were killed in a horrific accident. They were also fostering a few of the kids from the ranch for whom we simply hadn't been able to find permanent living solutions. It was a good thing the Warner Ranch was huge, because it was overrun with kids these days.

Rodie yawned again and followed me into the master bedroom. He was rubbing his eyes when he told me, "Cam sent a text that he's coming home for Christmas break. He wants to bring Ethan with him. He wanted to know if you would reach out and ask his mom and Grady if they wanted to come to the ranch for the holidays."

Rodie's yawn was contagious. I blinked and stretched my arms over my head. "Why didn't he ask me directly?"

Cam had graduated with honors and was currently in college in Colorado. We all thought he was going to want to go to school in a big city and move away from Wyoming when he got the chance, since he still stood out from everyone his own age in Sheridan. Instead, we'd all been pleased when he announced his interest in becoming a large animal vet. The demand was high where he lived, but the availability was minimal. We were all crazy proud of him, and we were secretly hoping he and Ethan could figure out how to make a real relationship work as they grew older and experienced more of what life had to offer together.

The boys talking, flirting, and falling for one another online had been one thing, taking their feelings out into a judgmental and often unpleasant public was another. Cam, of course, rolled with the punches, but Ethan wasn't made of the same unbreakable material as the former runaway. He told Cam he was bisexual, and tearfully admitted he was involved with a girl at his school right before the boys made plans to head to the same school after graduation. He claimed to really love the girl and apologized over and over again for leading Cam on. Ethan told Cam he wasn't ready to leave New York, and that he wasn't ready for anything serious with another boy. He was happy in his relationship, acknowledging it would be easier to stay with the girl. Of course, Cam was heartbroken, but in his typical fashion, he rallied and focused all his energy on graduating at the top of his high school class so he could go to the college of his dreams. Being at CU Boulder put him within driving distance of Sheridan and close to his brother. The laid-back vibe of the small college town suited him well. He was far from the only young gay man with neon hair and designer clothes on the big campus.

Cam started dating almost as soon as he began college. He instantly came out of his shell and fell into a routine of being just a regular college student. He was happy and his easy adjustment made Lane and Brynn breathe easy. Ethan didn't handle seeing pictures of Cam with other cute boys very well.

The other boy ended things with his high school sweetheart and transferred schools in the middle of a semester, much to my former partner's dismay. Ethan showed up on Cam's campus unannounced, immediately declared he'd made a horrible mistake, and loudly proclaimed his love. Cam was obviously skeptical after Ethan's previous actions, and he was still hurt by what he considered to be his betrayal. He didn't mind that Ethan was bisexual, but he was upset that he'd hidden the fact and lied to both him and the girl. He'd broken Cam's trust, and there was no way around that. The damage was done, and Cam was ready to move on.

But Ethan wasn't ready to give up. It took a full year for him to get Cam to agree to date. Now the boys were together, but their relationship had all the usual ups and downs of young love. Keeping up with them was exhausting, but that didn't keep Cam from texting me several times a day. Lane often joked that I heard from his oldest more than he did.

"I dunno why he asked me and not you directly. I told him I would pass the message along." Rodie blinked suddenly and fell backward onto the bed as I started to undress. I needed a shower and planned on asking him to join me. "Oh, maybe he asked me because he was asking how the task force investigation is going. He told me he keeps warning Opal about going out by herself at night."

Opal was Brynn's younger sister. She was a beautiful, headstrong girl with whom Cam was exceptionally close. Of course, he was worried about her with a rapist on the loose.

Rodie chuckled up at the ceiling. "He's still pissed she finally gave his idiot older brother a chance."

Cam's older brother Mikey had been in a pretty severe snowboarding accident last winter. Lane and Brynn brought him to the ranch to recover so they could keep an eye on him. Opal ended up helping him study to stay on track with school while he was laid up. Sparks flew, and the two had been an item ever since, much to Cam's dismay. His older brother had matured considerably over the years, but he was still kind of a screw up, and Cam fully believed Opal deserved better.

I shrugged out of my shirt and kicked the jeans off my long legs. I had full mobility back on most days. My shoulder still ached regularly, and I still had a slight hitch when I walked, but I no longer needed a cane to get around.

"How *is* the investigation going?" He didn't often bring his work home with him, but when he did, I made sure to pay attention.

Rodie swore and closed his eyes. "It's going nowhere. Everyone is too worried about stepping on jurisdictional toes. No one is sharing information freely. I'm going out to the reservation tomorrow to see if their law enforcement has any leads, since the last girl was abducted off their land. I doubt they'll be any more open to sharing, but I gotta try something."

"You'll figure it out."

I knew he would. He was a great cop and couldn't abide by anyone getting hurt on his watch. Now that we had a daughter of our own to protect, he had a new intensity toward doing good and keeping our town safe.

"If you need an extra set of eyes and ears, you know I'm here." I always appreciated it when he wanted to bounce ideas off of me. It meant all my years of training and deductive reasoning weren't going to waste. I might not carry a badge and gun anymore, but I was still involved in law enforcement.

I turned toward the bed; Rodie's eyes had closed and he seemed to be breathing smooth and deep. I hovered over him, grinning down at his ruggedly handsome face. Even heroes ran out of steam occasionally. I dropped a kiss on the center of his forehead and turned to go to the bathroom so I could shower away the day and join him in dreamland.

I gasped in surprise when strong arms suddenly wrapped around my waist and pulled me back. I landed on top of Rodie with an 'oomph' and a chuckle. His hands immediately skated over bare skin, and I could feel his body reacting underneath me.

"I'm glad you're home. I've missed you a lot lately."

We were both very busy trying our best to help so many others. We had to make a concentrated effort to give each other the time and attention our relationship deserved. We had to remain a united front no matter what came our way.

I stilled when I felt his big hand wrap around my twitching cock. "Missed you, too. Maybe after everyone gets together for Christmas and the weather clears up some, we should go away somewhere. Just me, you, and Eli."

Putting full sentences together was hard with his fist engulfing my erection, sliding up and down.

Rodie sighed. "I would love that."

I smiled into the darkness. "I love you." I really did. It snuck up on me, but I didn't regret giving him my heart. He always did his best to take care of it.

"I love you, too." He really did. He showed me in different ways every single day.

"This feels really good, but if you don't hurry it up, we're going to get interrupted." Eliana had impeccable timing when it came to interrupting her dads' alone time.

"Let's take a shower." I let Rodie shift me off of him and followed him as he got to his feet.

I winged up an eyebrow as I took his hand and followed him across the room. "Is that an order?"

He wiggled his dark eyebrows back at me and asked, "Do you want it to be?"

I kind of did. I liked it when he told me what to do while we had sex. "Yeah, I do. Tell me what you want me to do, and I'll do it."

Rodie stopped and turned to look at me, green eyes gleaming. "Stay with me forever."

That was his favorite demand, and I was more than happy to comply.

"I'm not going anywhere." There was nowhere else I'd rather be.

THE END

If you enjoyed the Getaway *series, be sure to check out my* Loveless *series as well!*

ACKNOWLEDGEMENTS

First of all, if you've made it this far in the book, thank you for your dedication. I'm still surprised, after this many books, that anyone cares what I have to say.

As I mentioned in the foreword, I never expected *Retreat* to bloom into a five-book series, but I'm glad it did. I think Rodie and Wyatt really bring everything full circle, and that they both really deserved a happy ending together. I had no idea writing cowboys would be so much fun, or so challenging, and oh my goodness, writing two big, tough alpha dudes kissing... maybe the best thing ever. I really do love a good male/male romance, and I will jump at any chance I get to write more of them. I always follow wherever my creative heart decides to go, and I sincerely appreciate the readers who wander with me. The destination is rarely ever known, but we have a really good time on our way. I appreciate those of you who ride or die with me, and I appreciate those of you who dip your toe in the water before deciding whatever I come up with next isn't for you. One book, or twenty... I have a deep love and respect for anyone who's shown up for me over the years.

Thank you to all the readers, bloggers, bookstagrammers, and reviewers who have taken a chance on this series just because my name is on the cover. I know it came out of left field, but honestly, how fun was this little literary experiment?! So fun!

Huge shout-out to my beta team. They went through it with this book. I was late. I wasn't making sense with the plot. My mind and the story were all over the place, but they got me back on track and helped me get a really lovely romance into the world. We were all under the gun, and I couldn't have pulled this story off without them. So, thank you with everything I have and all that I am: Pam, Alexandra, Sarah, Karla, Meghan, and Terri.

As always, I owe my super talented and mega-amazing girl-gang more than I can say. Mel is forever my favorite southern belle and the only reason I function most days. I couldn't ask for a better right-hand woman. My agent Stacey, who's been with me for all thirty books I've written and loves them all equally, is one of the reasons I'm brave enough to write whatever the hell I want. My professional team is unparalleled. If you want a beautiful book inside and out, go give them all your money. You won't regret it. All of their info is at the front of the book, but they almost should be on the front cover along with me. I wouldn't have a book to put in your hands if it wasn't for them. Elaine is a fantastic editor. Her insights are sharp and sure. She makes the guts of my book look as good as the outside. She's multitalented and a delight to work with. Hang is a design genius…full stop. There is no one better or brighter than she is when it comes to creating a stunning, unforgettable cover. Then there's Beth. My friend, and often my conscience and teacher. Even though she's years younger than me, I feel like I learn something new from her every single time I see her and with each and every book we work on together. And finally, a big thanks to Jessica from InkSlinger PR. She picked up the ball and kept running with my crazy pace when my former PR person left. It couldn't have been easy, but I'm very grateful she was up to the challenge.

Mostly, I just owe all I have to those of you who love reading romance so much. Even if you aren't reading my books in particular, it's still so awesome to see so many readers being well fed and thriving every single day. Loving books is a beautiful thing, and I'm forever thankful I get to have a place in the big, wild book world in any kind of way.

ABOUT THE AUTHOR

NEW YORK TIMES & USA TODAY BESTSELLING AUTHOR Jay Crownover is the international and multiple *New York Times* and *USA Today* bestselling author of the Marked Men series, The Saints of Denver series, The Point series, Breaking Point series, and the Getaway series. Her books can be found translated in many different languages all around the world. She is a tattooed, crazy-haired Colorado native who lives at the base of the Rockies with her awesome dogs. This is where she can frequently be found enjoying a cold beer and Taco Tuesdays. Jay is a self-declared music snob and outspoken book lover who is always looking for her next adventure, between the pages and on the road.

This is the link to join my amazing fan group on Facebook: https://www.facebook.com/groups/crownoverscrowd ... I'm very active in the group, and it's often the best place to find all the latest happenings including: release dates, cover reveals, early teasers, and giveaways!

My website is: www.jaycrownover.com... there is a link on the site to reach me through email. I would also suggest signing up for my newsletter while you're there! It's monthly, contains a free book that is in progress so you'll be the first to read it, and is full of mega giveaways and goodies. I'm also in these places:

https://www.facebook.com/jay.crownover
https://www.facebook.com/AuthorJayCrownover
Follow me @jaycrownover on Twitter
Follow me @jay.crownover on Instagram
Follow me on Snapchat @jaycrownover
https://www.goodreads.com/Crownover
http://www.donaghyliterary.com/jay-crownover.html

CPSIA information can be obtained
at www.ICGtesting.com
Printed in the USA
BVHW040204250722
642902BV00024B/85